DARK PROPHECY:

Rise of the Hunter

Barb Jones

Immortal Cravings Publishing, LLC

Venice, FL

LICENSING NOTES

Cover: Jarred Kern
Editor: Michel Martin del Campo

Library of Congress Control Number: 2023906430

DEDICATION

Ari & Kaiden: Words go without saying – Everything I do, I do for you.

Mom: Always my role model and best friend.

JoAnn Boothby & Constance Rose: Creators of Demons Eve and Garnet Rose, readers who became friends of mine.

ARC Team: Thank you for being part of this book and spreading the word about the series and me.

AUTHOR'S NOTE

I am personally humbled and excited to bring this book to my readers. It not only focuses on the Tall Dark Man in the series but I introduce a lot of new witches and demons. Two demons you will meet in this book are the creations of two readers – Constance and JoAnn, who won an exclusive contest! It was a great honor for me to work with them.

I will share my heritage with you in Rise of the Hunter through the kama'āina gods and some of my ancestors. I descend from a long line of kahunas going back to Ancient Hawaii and it is a great pleasure of mine to introduce you to some of them in this book. Please enjoy as the world of Blood Prophecy continues.

OTHER WORKS BY BARB JONES

BLOOD PROPHECY SERIES
QUEEN'S DESTINY
QUEEN'S ENEMY
QUEEN'S ASCENSION

BLOOD PROPHECY NOVELLAS
AMBER: BIRTH OF A QUEEN
CHLOE: VISIONS OF THE FUTURE
MARCUS: ORIGINS
MACHIEL: STONE OF THE DAMNED
ZARAQUEL: MORAL COMPASS

HENRY AND ANNE: A TUDOR LOVE STORY

COMING SOON

THE SHERIFF, THE DRIFTER, AND THE WHORE:
DEAL WITH THE DEVIL

THE DEVIL INSIDE ME

THE CURSE OF MARY

HEAVEN AND HELL SERIES
HELL HOUNDS (BOOK 2)

AN INTRODUCTION TO SOME HAWAIIAN WORDS:

O'hana – Family

Wahine – Female, Woman

Mahalo – Bye, thanks

Aloha – Hi, Welcome

Tūtū – Grandparent

Keike – Child

Kaimoni – Demons

Kama'āina - Hawaiian

AN INTRODUCTION TO PIDGIN WORDS:

Pidgin is spoken in Hawaii and comes from the Hawaiian language as well as other Polynesian languages.

Aunty – a female role model,
not necessarily related to you

B52 Bombah – large
cockroach

Bumbai – later on or else

Da Kine – "that kind"

Grinds – meal

Howzit – how locals greet
each other, "how's it going?"

Kden – "Ok, then"

Lolo – crazy, dumb, goofy

Ono – describes food as
delicious

Slippah – slipper, shoe

Uncle – a male role model,
not necessarily related to you

CAST OF CHARACTERS

The Tall Dark Man – His real name is known to only a few, his power is evil and he controls the demons and dark magic.

Amber – The queen who united the supernaturals and rules over them with justice and loyalty.

Chloe – The strongest light witch in the world.

Marcus – A vampire with a loyal heart.

Malakai – The alpha wolf with a strong heart.

Raven – Descendant from the line of Hexham Witches.

Zaraquel – The Avenging Angel, daughter of Chloe and Marcus.

Anne – The dark witch with the power to teach dark magic to Zaraquel.

Nimue – Friend to Zaraquel, who now serves the light.

Prologue

Sisters of Fate, Greece 1129 B.C.

The Sisters of Fate controlled the fate of humans. Clotho weaved while Lachesis determined their destiny. Clotho had finished weaving the life of a young girl named Diana when she was interrupted by an appearance from the temple's oracle.

"Clotho, as leader of the Sisters, I request an audience to speak about the prophecy."

Clotho motioned for the oracle to come forward and sit among the sisters of fate. She noticed Lachesis was not pleased with the oracle's presence, and Atropos couldn't care. She reached for her sisters and had them put the thread of Diana down.

Clotho said, "Come forward, oracle. I sense the child you wish to speak about. Her thread is in our hands, but we don't know her fate, and Lachesis has not decided it yet."

The oracle smiled. "I am not late. Behold the prophecy and turn of events. I merely serve the prophecy with my sight of the future."

The Sisters of Fate gathered around the oracle, and Clotho pushed the prophet to continue. She was impatient to know humans' destinies, especially the children, and Clotho knew the child's fate hung in the balance once the oracle halted the threading and allotting.

The oracle spoke.

"The prophecy has two sides, tangled in a battle that will span a millennium. The girl's thread, there in your hands, is special. The prophecy marks her as the messenger. A seer of the temple. She is Diana, is she not? Her mother is a mortal, but her father is one of the prophecy's servants. Her destiny will be to serve the prophecy by finding the blood drinker, a keeper, and telling him of the queen's arrival. Alas, there is another child. A twin. Have you threaded him yet?"

Clotho looked suspiciously at the oracle but didn't say a word. Instead, she waited for the prophet to reveal more. But the prophet remained silent. Finally, Clotho couldn't take the silence any longer and said, "Continue, please."

The oracle smiled at Clotho and her sisters and said, "The boy. The son of evil. He has an older, darker soul. One that has no beginning, but the end is unknown. There are three prophecies, not one, out in the mortal world. The first prophecy – the first battle – has already taken place. The second prophecy tells of the battle in which the child Diana will speak in the ancient tongue. The third prophecy – the ultimate battle – will be the one the boy serves for all time as he grows into a man, or at least until another child reaches her purification and faces him. The purified child will either win against his evil nature or become his bride, and evil will unleash to the world."

Clotho had to think for a moment. She did not expect to hear about hell on earth and what would happen to the Sisters of Fate if this son won. She needed to know more. She needed to secure the Sisters' destinies and purpose for the lives of all humans.

"This prophecy you speak of. Will it replace the Sisters?"

The oracle looked straight into her eyes. "The prophecies do not replace the Sisters of Fate. You need to thread the lives until the right ones serving the prophecy come along. Only you will know their fate. But the son must live as an immortal to fulfill the prophecy, and he will always be known as evil. The daughter, Diana, must die to be reborn again and again as a servant of the prophecy. With each new life, Diana will serve those who belong to the prophecy in ways no one will discover. She will be unimportant to the world except to those who are part of the prophecy."

With that, the oracle left the sisters, and Clotho had many more questions but no one to ask. She faced her sisters and began threading the human lives. The fates decided for the son and the daughter.

Chapter One
Dark Promises

The Tall Dark Man, The Pit, Three Years ago

The Tall Dark Man fell into the shadows while listening to the screams of the other victims. He still called upon his dark magic to save him as he fell. He could never cease to exist. This was not possible. He is the one that serves the darkness, while The One helps the light. While falling into nothingness, he called upon the darkest of magic to steal all the powers from the other victims.

Let them die. They mean nothing to me anymore, he thought.

After sensing Elizabeth and Mona nearby, he drained them of their life force but left enough in Elizabeth to keep her alive. Mona may survive, but it would take years to restore her power. Punishment for failing him. He may have been a man of darkness, but he kept his promise to his favorite witch. He continued to draw on the life forces of others to regain his strength; he shouted enchantments. The pit was a portal with its purpose, its own will. The pit supported neither side. Somehow, the pit obeyed his will and spat him out violently. Then the pit released Elizabeth and Mona. It expelled people, barely breathing, but at least alive.

Once the pit regurgitated him, he set his sights on a new plan. He knew the red-headed queen had claimed victory, forcing him to begin anew. She was the fool who didn't quite understand the prophecy, but since he had existed for centuries, he knew the sign was incomplete. With his hat covering his face once more in its usual fashion, but this time a little lower to hide the scar he received in the battle, he decided it was time to create a formidable army that would not be destroyed. The time was not right to chase her. His army needed to search the world for his lost stone.

A stone that Machiel took from him centuries ago.

First, he needed to return to the beginning where things started. The river where Krieg was born. He needed only one stone from that river to create this new army. Once the stone was in his possession, he embarked on a little trip; he arrived at the Hawaiian Islands.

***

The Hawaiian Gods, Hawaiian Islands, Three Years Ago

The four Hawaiian Gods, Kāne, Kū, Lono, and Kanaloa, sat along the volcano's rim, waiting for this stranger to communicate with them. Kāne, the God of Sky and Creation, was the one brother that ranked higher than Kū and Lono. Kāne was the Chief God of the Hawaiian trinity, and Kanaloa was the god that complemented him by holding power over the oceans. The gods watched over the land and its people before they saw the stranger. They followed him as he turned over lava rocks, digging his fingers into the earth, which made Lono, the god of agriculture and peace, look disgusted. Kū did not enjoy seeing his brother this way.

The stranger, not a native of the islands, continued to walk up the volcano until he reached the rim where they sat. With a raise of his hand, Kāne stopped him from walking closer. Kū, the God of War, sensed something familiar about this stranger. The gods all shared the same thoughts and feelings when they were together. The four were like one unless separated into parts of the island.

Kū motioned his hand to the ground, forcing the stranger down on his knees. He stretched his hand over the stranger's head, closed his eyes, and chanted. The stranger was forced into reverence as Kāne, Lono, and Kanaloa approached.

Kāne was the first god to speak. "Stranger, you invade our land and its people with your foul stench. What is it you look for from this land?"

The stranger could not speak their language, but they allowed him to understand it using their powers. The stranger understood what was asked, reached into his coat pocket, and pulled out a stone. He raised the stone to the gods, and using his mind, he told them about needing the hottest fire possible to finish his plan. He told them the prophecy, and the war was divided into three parts. The stranger spoke about the five heroes and that because of them, he sought vengeance. Kū sensed the power in this stranger and offered him salvation. He embraced the stranger, and a bond was formed between them. But Kāne, Lono, and Kanaloa were surveillant but powerless as Kū helped the stranger.

Kū and the stranger left for Kū's part of the Hawaiian Islands. He noted death, plague, and pestilence in this man. The man was searching for something. Then Kū remembered the fire. He summoned Tūtū Pele, Goddess of the Volcanoes and Fire. One of the most beautiful goddesses of the Hawaiian Islands. She approached Kū as a beautiful young maiden but changed her form to an older woman as Kū introduced the stranger.

"Pele, this is the stranger to our islands. He searches for the hottest fire the earth can produce, which is the Volcano Fire. He is no ordinary mortal and a man of dark evil with a story to tell. I think you will enjoy his tale."

At that point, the stranger spoke, and Kū made it possible for him to talk to both gods in their language.

***

The Tall Dark man looked at the god Kū and smiled. His basic features were kept hidden. He spoke to the god, and in his mind, he kept his true purpose hidden.

"Kū, is it? And you are Pele. I come in search of the hottest fire to breathe life into this stone, and this stone will breathe life into others. If you are the goddess of volcanoes and fire, you could help me."

He watched the goddess and the god talk it over, and Kū spoke. "We will help, but you will owe us a favor. We will call upon you because this act will anger the other gods. Pele senses something about you. We will need you one day to pay your debt for this act of kindness shown to you. Follow her and seek your fire. It would help if you left immediately and only returned when your debt is returned to the Kama'āina Gods. You, stranger, serve us now."

The Tall Dark Man nodded in acquiescence and gritted his teeth while he hid his true intentions. While the queen enjoyed her time of peace, he planned his return. Pele led him to the heart of her volcano and showed him the pit of fire. As she spoke to him, he could see her beauty. Once he had the stone, he searched her eyes for any sign of attraction, and there was none. She took the stone from him without asking and tossed it into the fire. He shouted in fear that the stone would be lost. He found the stone in his hand after it fell into the fire. It wasn't hot from the fire, but he could sense a burning odor from the rock.

"Stranger, the heat will not harm you. This volcano fire turns to ash, but with your stone, it will not. The fire is within the stone. Summon the fire when you need it. But what is this stone? It is strange looking."

He smiled at her question. "This stone is new. I used to have five stones until I lost them. This stone, however, I created from a demon who once served me.

I need a demon like him. His name was Krieg. With this stone, I will create a formidable army of demon fire warriors intent on destruction. With her help, I will find a particular stone lost to me a long time ago. The stone is needed to find others. I thank you, Tūtū Pele, for your most generous gift. I must bid you farewell to continue my search. I shall stay on your islands just a while longer."

And with that, he took his leave from her volcano and searched the land for more ancient signs to help him create his army.

***

The Tall Dark Man, Underground, Present Day (Three Years Later)

The Tall Dark Man called forth his witches of great power. He called upon their spirits, regardless of flesh and blood. He owned their souls, and because of that, they lived to serve only him. Thirteen powerful witches stood before him. His coven. Tapping his right fingers on the stone armrest of his throne, his left hand cradled his chin. His chin, left crooked from falling in the pit, never straightened and distorted his face. As he looked over towards his coven of dark witches, he watched them as they bowed in reverence to him.

"My coven. I call upon you to create an army of demons from that stone. It is the oldest stone and can be bent to obey my will. Create this army using that stone as it holds the strongest and hottest fire in the world. It is a volcano fire. Give this army strength, cunning, and power, for it will have to rise against the queen, the angel Zaraquel, and the witch. This army can't be destroyed except by one word. I will give you that word when it is time."

The witches stood whispering in front of him. One of them dared to speak.

"And what names shall we give these demons? To know one's name is to command it."

"When the demons are ready, I shall name them myself. This way, there is only one master. Do you remember Krieg, the Stone Demon? These need to be even more vicious. Krieg was the perfect Stone Demon, but a vampire and his witch wife destroyed him. Raise my army or suffer my wrath. When you have succeeded, I have more tasks for you in the days ahead."

The same outspoken witch came to the Tall Dark Man and bowed to him. "Yes, lord. Your wish is our command."

He saw all the witches standing before him, bow in servitude, and retreat to create his army. However, the Tall Dark Man summoned one witch back to him. She was a dark-skinned woman, and he admired her beauty. She was one of his favorites because, despite her physical age, he ensured her youth and beauty. The witch would lie with many men and bear their children, instructing all of them about dark magic, and causing speculations during the trials. He saved her after her time in jail by replacing her with a demon molded into her image. The Tall Dark Man wasn't about to let anything happen to his witch after the Salem Trials. Not as strong as his sweet Elizabeth Hexham… Her loins bore him many demon sons and daughters.

She asked, "Will we create stone demons, or will there be more?"

The Tall Dark Man smiled and shifted his position on his throne. Motioning her to come forward, he grabbed her breasts and titillated them, stimulating her body in response to him. He watched her close her eyes and sway her hips, spreading herself open to him. His witches knew his needs and when to service him. This was one of those times… He grabbed her hair and pulled her head back, her back arched.

"You, my sweet Tituba, shall give birth to a hunter. A hunter whose only purpose is to kill the queen and bring me the avenging angel. He will rise from your womb. He will kill the queen and her pets and bring their lifeless bodies to me so that the coven can raise them from the dead and command them to serve me. Only the angel will be left alone."

Tituba nodded and replied, "I am honored, master. Will this hunter succeed? The last failed miserably, and you were in a terrible rage of anger."

Scratching his chin, he thought for a moment and answered her. "Yes, because through him, all the demons and beings that serve me will follow his command while he is on his mission. He won't be alone. Be calm. I won't make that mistake again. Now, concentrate on something else, my sweet." Then, he covered her with his body and implanted his seed into her womb.

***

Raven Hexham, Underground, Present Day

The outspoken witch stood before the coven, and they gathered around to listen to her. This witch was revered because of her power and status. She was a Hexham witch. When he found her, she accepted his calling because she was raised to answer him whenever he called. She went by the name Raven Hexham, and through her line, her mother taught her the craft from an early age. Raven was a direct descendant of Elizabeth Hexham's daughter Alison, who was gifted in witchcraft and handpicked by the Tall Dark Man to continue to bear his offspring. Raven was reborn through the generations, and with each passing, she could absorb an earlier witch's power into her own from a spell cast by Alison in the 1570s. Raven inherited her power and all those before her when her mother passed. Her strength and power were so raw and intense that they almost matched the intensity of Elizabeth Hexham. Raven was part of the new generation in her family. Although she felt a special connection to the master, he never sired his seed through her. She felt a sting of jealousy towards Tituba, but she saw how she would lose her strength and power after many births. He kept her pure and potent, more critical than motherhood to demons.

The other witches saw her strength and power, and none could match them. They allowed her to head up the coven. She wove the spells, and in the end, they all joined in, aiding her as she manipulated the one stone to become many. The stone was turned into many rocks. Reaching for the master stone, Raven held on to it and felt its power. From here, she and her coven could breathe life into the others. Raven could sense the fire from within, but the outer shell did not burn. Throwing this original stone in the air, her hands moved as if in a dance while she chanted a spell.

"Sisters, join me in this spell. Mimic your hands to mine. Repeat my words. It will take everyone to create the first demon. Hurry, while I have the stone bent to our will. Create! Create!"

The witches formed a circle, keeping Raven in the center, and the stone floated in the air. As their arms moved in sequence, their chant gave the stone life. Arms, legs, and two heads formed out of stone. The stone twisted and changed shape until, in the air, the coven floated a stone demon whose size and shape would scare anyone. Raven lowered the monster to the ground, where the witches whispered about him. He was not like the Stone Demon Krieg at all. He looked more terrifying. Raven walked up to him, and his eyes were closed. He was not yet alive. Holding her palm out under her chin, her lips formed a small circle, and she breathed into him.

The Stone Demon moved, exploring his new arms and raising his legs up and down. Raven moved around him with her right hand running over the stone texture of his massive body, admiring her artwork. He stood six foot seven, towering over her by a foot. His legs were strong, and she rubbed her fingers over his eyes, granting him sight beyond sight. Then, placing her cupped hands over his large ears, she whispered another spell, allowing him to hear everything. She motioned for him to kneel, and when he did, she placed her hands over his head and granted him the ability to obey the master's every command and wish without question. He was born to serve the master and lead his army. Now, the witches needed to make his army from the other stones.

Raven told the other witches to use the remaining stones. They worked together to make these stone soldiers as solid and formidable as he wanted. If the witches didn't, failure would be upon the coven. They continued to make the stone demon army for days and nights, working until the task was carried out. Once finished, the witches lay down on the cold ground. Raven noticed they were all smiling at their handiwork and praised her for her power and guidance. She earned her break before returning to the master.

Raven entered the master's throne room and saw Tituba sitting in a corner. Raven approached her witch sister and said, "How are you feeling? To carry the master's latest seed is a great honor."

Tituba looked at her and said, "It is, but I am tired. My spells are not working like they used to. I used to control the minds of others, but now I cannot. But this child, this hunter he calls it, is essential to his plans. Are you looking for him?"

Raven asked if she was happy doing this or would prefer to do something else. Tituba looked at her.

"Tituba, we are nothing more than servants to the master. On a day when your conscience will awaken, you might question what you're doing. Do you want to be the master's broodmare? The witches don't give life to the same number of demons. Don't you want more power? To see the outside world? It's been centuries since you have been here, and you can't even go anywhere without a chain wrapped around your body. Why do this to yourself, Tituba?"

Tituba let a tear fall, and she nodded to Raven. She wanted her life to be free.

Before Raven could say anything, the master summoned her to his presence.

"Do you have my army? Why did it take so long?"

Raven smiled, wanting to keep her favor with him. "Master, I had the coven working day and night to create the army. I breathed life into the leader while the other demons were under his command. And he is to follow only you. It is what was breathed into him to give him life. He knows no other; he will follow no other. Your army awaits your command, but you must name them all before that can be done. Knowing their name will give you ultimate power over them. Come, let me introduce your new army."

The master followed her into the room where the army stood, waiting for his command.

***

Philip II, Hostage of Illyria, 368-365 B.C.

Philip II was a hostage sent to Illyria shortly after his older brother Alexander II was assassinated. Philip prayed for a way out of his predicament, feeling betrayed and used as a political pawn. He didn't remain long in Illyria because he was then sent to Thebes. Confined to his prison, he continued to think of ways to escape, though he was still a young boy.

A strong military leader named Epaminondas was interested in the boy because Philip II would tell him things. Philip II liked this soldier and saw how strategically his mind worked, and Philip II thought Epaminondas was the answer he was looking for. Epaminondas taught him military strategy during one of their visits, claiming he would win battle after battle.

"See, boy; I swore fealty to a powerful man. I don't even think he's a man, but I swore my loyalty for as long as I continue to breathe, and he gives me victories. Do you see yourself as a military leader, a leader of nations, boy?"

Philip II thought about it for a second. "I want to conquer nations and avenge the man who sent me here."

Epaminondas smiled and sat on the ground near the boy. "I will call my master and let him show you the way."

Epaminondas called on the man with a dark hat. Philip only wanted out of Thebes and to look for his revenge. The man appeared and spoke to him.

Philip swore his loyalty and endured his time in Thebes while receiving a diplomatic education, and, in return, he would have nothing but success. It only cost him time to receive his education. Philip did not know what his loyalty would cost at this early age but agreed to return home.

The man looked at him and smiled. "You will take a wife; your daughters will carry my seed through them. My children will call the serpent and bend the will of men. They will be strong in the darkest magic. And sons that you have, through your wife, will be stronger military conquerors than you because you will train them to be military conquerors, overthrow the weakest men, and more. You will be remembered for serving me. One son must stay a mortal. If he loses his mortality, you will find your soul in permanent chaos and fire—all in due time, boy. I will return when you have sought your victories and claimed your wife. It is written."

"What do you mean, a mortal? What aren't you telling me?"

The man laughed and ruffled his hair. "The world has more than men—armies and legions of beings of great power which I command. I give you the gift of strength and the ability to win wars to take what I need. The one to remain mortal will earn the favors of men in time. That is all you need to know."

Philip didn't quite understand everything but wanted to be out of Thebes. He shook the man's hand.

Philip spent his time learning his military education and diplomacy from his friend Epaminondas, even when he was sent to live with one of Epaminondas' friends as a hostage of Thebes. He was no longer confined to prison. Instead, he was sentenced to serve in a worse situation. He began a relationship with Pammenes, a friend of Epaminondas. Though he suffered this fate, the man gave him unbelievable strength and determination to survive and learn his military education. Eventually, he earned his freedom and served the man he met all those years ago. His wife bore him many children just as the man told him.

Chapter Two
Family

Amber, The Estate in Seattle, Present Day

Since the death of Michael, Amber hadn't grasped the evil of the Tall Dark Man. She remained focused on training, collaborating with the wolves, and hunting with Marcus. Amber knew her role as the queen did not end with the battle. She felt a force pulling her into the library. It was never a strong pull until her birthmark grew hot. And this evening, her neck felt like it was on fire. Upon entering the library, her birthmark cooled. The room seemed more inviting to her. Amber had never visited the library since Michael's death. His death affected her, but the more she thought about it, the angrier she became because of his deception. She knew it wasn't Michael's fault, but she missed him.

Hmm, that is so strange, she thought to herself. Then she whispered, "Spirits of the past, show me what you want me to see."

The books on the shelf shook, and they fell to the ground individually. But one, in particular, fell and opened on its own. Amber was curious, so she kneeled before it, touching it, for she didn't know what to expect. It was wrapped in a velvet sack, so she opened it. She peered at the cover. On the cover was a gold triangle, and in the center was a red eye. The pages were written in an ancient language. Amber ran her fingers over the words and tried to pronounce a few she recognized but couldn't understand.

Placing her hand over her amulet, she closed her eyes and breathed. "I call onto you, lady of the prophecy. Could you guide me? I should be able to do this. I was once Bircenna, then Illyris. I am the queen. I should be able to read this." Amber became discouraged because nothing had happened. As she looked once more, however, she could read the words. It was a history book. She saw familiar names she remembered reading from before. The original book of the Romani clan. She couldn't believe it.

"Chloe! Chloe! Come to the library. Now. I found something."

Both Chloe and Malakai came running into the library. They gathered around Amber as she placed the book on the table.

"Geez, Amber, what did the library do to you?" asked Chloe.

"It just happened. I'll clean it up later. This book… it called to me."

Amber saw that Chloe ran her fingers over the cover and screamed. The book somehow wouldn't let her touch it. Amber realized the book had burned Chloe's hand. She reached for it and looked at the redness. Chloe bent closer to the book and nudged Amber to show her more. If Michael had it in his possession, she wondered how he touched it? She guessed that there would be many questions with no answers.

Malakai asked, "This is a fabulous find, Amber. But what is it?"

Malakai looked at both her and Chloe. Amber knew this look, and Malakai looked excited about this. He also tried to touch the book, but Amber moved his hand. She got comfortable on a velvet sofa with the book. The others crowded around her.

Amber said, "Here it is. The beginning talks about Eshmun'azar. It says that a young girl spoke the ancient prophetic language and spoke about a queen. That must mean me. But, later, it says that he found another set of scrolls older than the ones about the girl. I'm not good with these ancient languages… and I'm not Michael." Her voice broke as she remembered her once lover with kindness and then remembered Machiel, the beast he became. Her heart missed him, though she loved Malakai.

Chloe placed her hand on Amber's shoulder, and it comforted her. Amber heard her say, "Try. It is all we can do. If we can't read this book, we will find someone who can. Someone connected to the prophecy must read the book. I was expecting another boring Saturday."

Amber took another deep breath and skimmed the pages. She read what she could. The others were so fascinated that they didn't hear Jerome come in.

"Dinner is served. We each have desires, but the table is set for all."

Amber looked up from the book and spoke to Jerome. "How long were you with Michael? Can you tell us what you know about this book? Do you know more about Kabos? We have a million questions!"

"Miss Amber, I will happily share all I know, but we should do it over a delicious dinner. The dining room is prepared. Shall we?"

He bowed and left so that they would follow him.

"We better follow him if we want our answers. Plus, it's fresh blood. Yum!" said Amber as she took the book to the dining room.

As everyone sat around the table. Amber noticed they were a family. Of course, seats were empty as Marcus, McPherson, Nimue, and Zaraquel were away. Marcus went searching for the girls because something was amiss. Amber worried for them all. When Michael was here, Amber noticed they didn't have family dinners, but Jerome ensured dinners were eaten together since his death. Jerome and others kept their positions, but Amber insisted that nothing ever be formal again. This became the rule when they learned Michael left everything to her and Marcus. However, Marcus turned his share over to her as he and Chloe wanted to settle near her coven one day.

Jerome told them what he knew. As Amber listened, she realized Jerome might have the answers to all their questions, but first, she remained quiet to hear his story.

"We were told stories of how our family served Kabos over the years. I thought these were fairy tales to put us to sleep, but I knew they were the truth once I met Michael because it was my turn to serve him. Kabos has employed my family for centuries, though we don't share in their vampiric nature. We keep our humanity to oversee things they could not. We are the keepers of family secrets. The book has chosen you for a reason, Amber."

Chloe's face made her laugh. Amber wasn't the only one perplexed.

Amber said, "Can you tell us more? Chloe looks like she will die without this information, and well, I'm already dead."

Jerome chuckled and continued.

"Kabos was one of the ancient ones. He was a Romani. Then he was turned. Like you, Miss Amber. But the prophecy chose him, his family, to guard it through his mother's line. His mother's people have always been the guardians. The book is the original history of the Romani prophecy: the whole prophecy, or at least a substantial portion of it. Michael was looking for certain pages. These pages are in different sections. This book was something Michael gave up on because of his transformation. The book wants you to pick up where he left off."

Amber smiled. She looked at Malakai and said, "We will all find its missing pages."

***

Birna, Venice, Italy, 1593

Birna and Xanto settled in their new home, and a babe would soon be cradled in her arms. It had been years since she left her people and their ancient ways, and Birna had set up their home with all the comforts and items that Xanto loved. He was a proud man, and things weren't always blissful when he discovered her true nature. As she cradled her bump, she felt nauseated and sat down.

As she ran her hand over her belly, she dreamed of the day Xanto admitted his love. Her dream soothed the stirring baby and brought her a sense of peace.

Xanto saw her walking along a trail in the woods and hopped off his horse. She didn't turn around or do anything to notice him. Instead, she stopped, opened her pack, and laid out a blanket. Birna glanced up at him and motioned for him to sit down. She spoke to him of her people and his great purpose. Xanto ignored the first part, but as they talked, she sensed a great power within him. Not long after, they began seeing each other more often.

Birna fell in love with him instantly and told him of her vision. Xanto said he was in love with her. Xanto asked Birna to be his wife. Then, Birna told him of the exceptional child that would one day be theirs.

She remembered the day they fell in love, and the baby inside her kicked as if he understood her memory, too. She hadn't considered her family in a long time. As the baby continued to kick, she called for Xanto, and he came running.

"Dear husband, the babe won't wait. It is time…." Before she could finish, Birna's eyes fluttered, and she spoke to Xanto in a strange voice.

"Xanto, husband of the great seer. Your son will be born, and his destiny is great. Teach him your ways, and Birna will teach him the ways of the Seers. Birna is from an ancient line of foretellers who are prophecy keepers. Remember. Speak these words to Birna once the child is born: 'Thou has the gift of sight. It never abandoned you.' Teach him the old ways. He will receive the book of prophecy. The gift is strong in him. The prophecy awaits your son and will call upon him when it's time. His name is to be Kabos."

Birna screamed. The baby was coming. Xanto helped her the best he could; before she knew it, the son was born. As she continued to labor in breath, Xanto told her what had happened, and a tear fell on her right cheek. Xanto had told her that the child would have the name Kabos. She saw Xanto fall to the ground on his knees and tell her he would protect them from anything and anyone looking to destroy them. He honored Birna by always promising to love her.

Birna tried to be brave. "I hear you, keepers of the truth. I will honor my heritage and do what is asked. The father has named the child."

Birna and Xanto found a routine that blessed them not only as parents of this unique child but also protected her legacy, and she loved her little family.

***

The birth of Pele, Hawaiian Goddess, Hawaiian Creation

Pele, born to the King of Tahiti, had an unruly temper, and because of indiscretions with her brother-in-law, she was banished and sent elsewhere. By canoe, she sailed to the Hawaiian Islands. Pele was beautiful, and her moods were unpredictable. One day, Pele spotted her sister Namakaokahai, and the two argued and fought.

Pele, beautiful and fiery, was no match for her sister. Her sister left because Pele did not move. Pele asked for her strength to stand and live by praying to the Sky Father. Because she was descended from the Sky Father, he granted her wish, and Pele recovered. She then fled to the other islands, and because of her temper, she created several fire pits by digging to stay alive. Pele traveled from island to island and loved the land's beauty.

One day, she saw her sister once more.

"Namakaokahai, leave me alone. Or you will regret it."

"Pele, you will die for sleeping with my husband."

Pele and Namakaokahai fought, and soon, Pele was no match again for her sister. The fight was a death match, and Pele died after being torn to pieces by her sister. Before her last breath, Pele called out to the Sky Father for life. The Sky Father responded by floating the dismembered pieces of Pele to the heavens, and, soon, Pele the Fire Goddess was born.

"You are now called Madame Pele, the god of fire. Through you, you will create or destroy the land before you. The hottest of fires will obey you. You will honor those that cherish the land. People are going to seek this land. Remember these words: Ua Mau Ke Ea o ka 'Āina I ka Pono. People must love the land, and you will show them how."

Madame Pele, now a goddess, wandered the land in search of other gods. As she roamed, the volcano fire obeyed her. She was an old lady or a young lady. She taught the people to love the land because the Sky

Father had warned her what would happen if they didn't. Madame Pele fell in love with the people.

***

The Tall Dark Man, Underground, Present Day

Looking at his new army, he was overly impressed with their strength. Once again, Raven did not fail him. He took his time naming each demon to keep power over them. The Tall Dark Man came to the demon who would be the leader of his stone army. Placing his hand on the head of this stone demon, he whispered his name.

"Arioch. Demon of vengeance. A fitting name for you. You will serve me well. When I call on you, you will lead your army of demons and seek vengeance on those who try to stop me. You will return to me when the task is done and wait until I have the next task for you."

Arioch came to life and kneeled before him with fealty. The Tall Dark Man honored him with his first task.

"Bring me the one they call Malakai. He is the wolf, a powerful one and closest to the queen. He will be most useful to me. Serve me well, Arioch."

The demon rose and left after the Tall Dark Man gave his command. Turning his attention to Raven, his most powerful witch, he gave her a wicked smile and said, "You have pleased me, Raven. I have another request for you. I was hoping you could find a particular book and bring it to me. The book was in Machiel's possession. It is with the queen now or one of her pets. You may play with them. Send them on a chase. I don't care but bring me that book."

Raven smiled and nodded. "Of course, master. I live to serve you. What about the coven?"

"Leave them to me. Vengeance against the queen and her pets will be mine. Prepare to leave at once. But do not let yourself be swayed by their light ways. You are powerful but have one weakness since I have not allowed you to carry my seed. Don't listen to their untruths. If you fail me, your life will be lost. I will have my vengeance." He left at once.

***

Raven Hexham, Seattle, Present Day

Raven walked the streets of Seattle, getting familiar with the people, the sounds, and everything. Being underground certainly had privileges because the people walking downtown were simply crazy to her. Walking along Pier 62, she was mesmerized by everything she saw. She eventually found herself in the downtown area. The number of homeless people on the street horrified her, but she assumed it was the aftermath of the battle.

She continued making her rounds through the different side streets until she smelled the familiar smell of dogs in human form. As a witch, Raven had ideal gifts that allowed her to sense when other races were nearby. Her servitude to the master increased her power and lowered her weaknesses against her enemies. Raven recalled the master telling the coven that the queen and her pets, as he called them, worked in the Seattle Museum of History and Art.

She found its location quickly. Walking through the front entrance, she approached the first person she saw and said, "I am Raven. I am here to see Malakai Ridgewater, which is significant to my donation."

She felt that the woman looked at her with disgust. Their eyes locked as each woman stared the other down for about a minute. As the woman turned to walk away with a slight moan, Raven smiled sweetly as she placed a wicked hex on the woman. She would be dead on this day. Raven waited for twenty minutes until a man appeared in front of her. She could smell his stench, and as it made her nauseated, she realized he also had an aura.

"I am Mr. Ridgewater. You asked to see me."

"Yes, I am Raven. Do you know who I am?"

"I believe I can't recall the pleasure, Miss Raven. How can I help you?"

As he extended his hand to her, she gripped his hand tightly and pulled close enough to him to whisper her first message.

"I serve the Tall Dark One, paramour to the queen. He sends you greetings. I am watching you and will come for you, stinking dog."

She felt him trying to release his hand from her grip, which only caused her to grip it harder.

> *"I am the mistress of the dark.*
> *I am the raven of the night.*
> *I call upon the ancient power.*
> *Curse this dog upon changing.*
> *He will walk on all fours.*
> *The kiss of his love will not break.*
> *For I hold the key to his undoing."*

She smiled at him and released his hand, saying, "I will see you soon. You can count on it."

She turned on her heels, walked out, and continued her plan. As she reached the street, she glanced down the dark alley. She saw Arioch, the stone demon, hiding in the shadows. Nodding to him, she sent him the message that Malakai was now cursed and easy for him to find. She disappeared to search for the book.

***

Pahulu, God of Nightmares, Ancient Hawaii

The island of Molokai was the hotbed for sorcery and nightmares since the god Pahulu succeeded the goddess Pahulu. Pahulu was both god and goddess until the god overpowered the goddess. The goddess was less frightening than the god; he turned dreams into nightmares and became the chief of ghosts and evil spirits. Pahulu wandered the land of Lanai, raising the spirits of the dead, causing the island to be overrun before returning to Molokai.

The god Kū visited Pahulu unannounced, and he did not like surprises.

"You come to my island and disturb my spirits. Why? Just because you are a powerful god?"

Kū laughed at him and replied, "Foolish little god. We were hoping you could create more spirits that roam the islands. The kahuna Lanikaula is getting too powerful. He will destroy you. But we have an idea. Let him find you when he empties his waste by the rock; he will think he killed you. He's destroying your followers. There will be a fish waiting. It will help if you become one with the fish. The people who eat the fish will come under your possession. We want you to collect the souls of those who eat the fish and for you to create your army of spirits. In return, you will honor me, the god Kū."

Pahulu, a lower god, agreed, and the next time Lanikaula went to the sacred rock to dispose of his excrement, he made sure the kahuna saw him. Pretending to drink, Pahulu could sense Lanikaula sneaking up on him. He allowed himself to be pushed into the water, connecting with the waiting weke in the water. Pahulu became one with the weke, and every time the fishermen caught the weke to eat, he possessed them and slowly watched from the waters as the fishermen became his army of evil spirits.

He looked up one day and saw Kū smiling at him, nodding in pleasure. Pahulu succeeded in his promise to Kū.

***

Amber, Seattle, Present Day

Amber and Chloe returned to the library to look through the book. Amber asked Chloe not to touch it. Amber begged her to find a spell to nullify the book's power. Chloe tried, with no success. As Chloe said the spells, Amber noticed her hands were turning red. Amber studied the book's behavior. She still couldn't understand why she could touch the book but Chloe's hands burned.

"I wonder, Chloe, if it isn't responding because you're a witch, and this is a Romani book. That would make sense. We should read more of the book, but try not to touch it."

Amber turned each page and marveled as the words started to make sense.

"Here it is, and it's a passage about the prophecy. Give me a minute to sort through this. The whole situation seems strange."

Amber read briefly before saying, "It would be known in the beginning. This was the Battle of the Beginnings. The dark and light would fight to control the world, destroying the races. The fight would decide which master they would serve. Do you know what that means, Chloe? This prophecy was already in play long before I became queen."

Chloe was ecstatic, so Amber continued to read.

"The queen will unite the races in a second battle. Blah blah, been there, done that." She kept reading.

"There is a third battle. Fuck, Chloe, not another one. This is like torture. But the Fates hold the answer according to the Romani prophecy. This is a wild goose chase! Look here - it's about a stone. The Tall Dark Man must never have possession of this stone. According to the Romani people, these stones will influence the fifth stone. Chloe, I can only summarize the words in this book to make sense. We need a real Romani to read it, I think. The only Romani Michael ever talked about was Kabos."

Chloe looked like a kid in the candy store. "Amber, we can call my coven, and they might know about this book. You keep reading while I make the call. We must make sense of it all. And it looks like we have a battle coming. Does it say how we will know?"

Amber shook her head and said, "No. We need to prepare somehow, all of us. Let me keep reading. Just listen, ok? Who knows what we will learn?"

Amber kept reading and skimming through the pages until she found a folded paper in the book. It was Michael's handwriting. She opened it up and inspected it; it appeared to be a letter written not long ago. She read the letter aloud.

My dearest Amber,

If you are reading this, then you will have opened this book. This book made its way to me long ago, and I can feel the darkness closing in on my soul as I write this. I am losing who I am and becoming what I once was—Machiel. But I am Michael as I write you this last letter. Never have I loved another the way I love you. I am sorry I was not strong enough. I knew the stone's hold on me would one day be my downfall.

I have never spoken to anyone of this stone— the stone of the damned. Only Kabos knew of my plight and burden for centuries. If you are reading this, then I am dead by your hand. You must find the stone. I have hidden the stone in the estate. The book will guide you if you tell it. There is another letter that will require my family to solve its riddle. The stone and the book are connected but should be in separate locations unless needed. This was done to keep the artifacts safe from evil. Use the book to find the stone. It will guide you if you believe. You are worthy. Evil must never get either. Stay brave, my faithful and rightful queen. Marcus, Chloe, and the others will protect you. Forgive me, my love, Mí Amor, for turning against you. I was too weak to resist the evil that took me from you. If you can't forgive me, I understand this as well.

Search my desk in my study. I have hidden something that will prove most valuable to you. This prophecy is more than we thought. Only Kabos, one keeper of the prophecy, knows the truth. Look for him and ask. We should have realized that this prophecy does not end, Mí Amor.

When you find the stone, call upon the ghost of Kabos. Jerome will aid you.

Till we meet again, Mí Amor,
Michael

By the time Amber finished reading the letter, both women were in tears. His words moved Amber because the honest Michael wrote them, and he loved her. She needed to figure out how the book would guide her to the stone. And how was she going to keep it safe?

***

Nostradamus, Italy, 1555

Nostradamus completed his next almanac and was excited to share it. He noted that this almanac spoke about different prophecies that would horrify the world. It was hard to fathom that he could have such thoughts. The images included destruction, the world ending, war, and more.

He wrote his various prophecies with each almanac and noticed that whenever he was out in public, people would whisper as if he didn't hear them. "He worships the devil," "He is evil," and the comments continued. Dismayed by the people's lack of knowledge, he somehow wished to prove them wrong.

He continued walking until he saw a little boy with dark hair who looked lost. The little boy looked hungry and was skin and bones. Nostradamus also noticed the boy was dirty and disheveled but appeared unharmed. Nostradamus approached him and offered him some bread and part of his eaten apple from his pack. It isn't much, as I ate most of it earlier, but I'm happy to share, young lad."

The boy looked up and smiled. "Can I show you something, sir? I promise it won't take long, and I will get lost afterward."

Nostradamus laughed and nodded. The little boy extended his hand, and he took it. Even though his little hand felt cold and odd, Nostradamus held it and let the little boy guide him. They walked awhile until the little boy stopped in a deserted alley. The little boy looked up at him and smiled, then turned into a goat. Nostradamus rubbed his eyes in disbelief. The goat changed. A young man with dark hair down to his broad shoulders and equally dark eyes stood before him.

Nostradamus finally said, "What sorcery is this? This cannot be!"

The young man chuckled. "I know who you are, Nostradamus. You don't know me yet. But you will. I've watched you. You share prophecies. I can do more for you, and I can gift the special abilities that will make those around you be moved by your gifts. They will follow you; they will believe you."

Before the young man could continue, Nostradamus was in shock. He wanted to avoid getting caught practicing magic. He said, "What abilities? I don't want to get caught up in heresy."

The young man laughed. "I can show you things you don't see. In return, there are certain people I want you to share these gifts with. You will impress people, and they will be in awe, all in return for obeying my wishes."

Nostradamus thought about this for a moment. No killing, no crime. Simple astrology and prophecy. "I must know who you are. It should scare me that you changed forms, but it doesn't, and it intrigues me."

"You will see me occasionally, and I will follow your exploits. You can't tell anyone else my name. I am called many things, but you can call me Sammael."

"I'm glad to have made your acquaintance, Sammael. Where shall I journey to send this message of yours?"

"She will summon you to Paris. Her name is Queen Catherine. Go to her. In time, my message will be received because she is the messenger. She awaits your arrival, and everything has been made ready."

***

Tall Dark Man, Underground, Present Day

He sat on his throne, watching his coven of witches creating his formidable new army. The Tall Dark Man didn't rush his planning since he wanted to ensure his vengeance and hold over the angel would resonate. The queen was crucial last time. She had to unite the races and all that prophecy nonsense to defeat him. The bitch was irrelevant to his new plans. She might interrupt the smoothness of his plans only if Raven and Arioch failed their tasks. She would not undo his plan, nor would she remain alive. He laughed as he thought about the unusual ways she would die. He mused at how the queen would be dead, once the angel was his. The thought of this made him smile. Once free from the pit, the Tall Dark Man could sense her, but he cloaked himself so she could not sense him. She lived in her beloved peace, but he laughed because he knew her peace was ending. He planned to leave her alone, for now, until the timing was right.

He glanced at his witches before visiting Tituba. He kept her in a secluded room once he was positive she had conceived. He closed the door upon entering the room.

"Tituba, my little concubine. I hate chaining you, but you have become too willful and defiant. I fear for your safety, and you've been looking unwell lately.

He touched her cheek and placed a hand on her womb. He could sense the tiny seed taking hold of her. He never understood why she became defiant when she bore him so many sons and daughters. His paranoia might get the best of him. The Tall Dark Man felt she was pretending to be in favor of bearing this demon child, but he couldn't understand why. She was the mother of his demon children all these centuries. The change in her attitude was annoying him.

"Oh, master, I am obedient," she said as she tried to wiggle free from the chains that held her captive. "I want to bear the hunter. It's an honor, and it's just… it's just that I heard things from others…"

Before she could continue, he stroked her cheek and seethed in anger. His eyes squinted as he eyed her up and down. Tituba had never lied to him before, but he could sense something different about her but couldn't quite figure it out. He blamed the queen for his paranoia. The way she protected her family and the avenging angel. His angel. Or at least his soon-to-be angel if the queen was dead. It was all a matter of time.

Before he could think about his next steps, Tituba screamed in pain. Her body writhed in agony as she twisted and turned while shackled. She was the first witch to lose his seedling. He felt the loss of his child;

the feeling hit hard, but he shook it off. He did not need his witches to think of him as a weakling.

"Tituba, what happened? You've always carried my seeds. Did you plot something to prevent my newest hunter?"

Tituba looked at him and denied it. "There was something wrong. The pain…" Her voice trailed off, and then she screamed.

He put her hand on her belly and mumbled several words. The hunter was gone from her womb. It didn't hold. Why? Furious, he clenched his hands into fists and stormed out of the room, leaving Tituba alone in agony. He marched straight to the library where he kept all his books and scrolls on the prophecy. He searched for a particular book that spoke about a Dark Prophecy. He couldn't find what he wanted. Then she walked in. *Ah*, he thought. *Mary. Valentine's wife. The dead hunter.* But he looked at her. So pretty. She was his toy, and now that his favorite hunter was dead, he had no use for her, but he enjoyed tormenting her.

"What do you want, Mary? I'm not interested in what you need now."

Mary quivered at the sharp tone he gave her. "I heard from the other witches that Valentine's dead. Since my husband is dead, why not just let me go? Let me live in the afterlife with him. Please. I beg you, master."

"I've told you every time you have asked for your freedom. No. You are mine, and here you will stay. Valentine's death does not change this. Now leave me be."

He kept searching until he came across an old scroll. It was written by both him and the True One. Looking at the scroll, he remembered that this was only half. The other half was with his nemesis. He remembered fighting with the True One, causing the scroll to be torn into two. He lost track of the details from long ago but swore he would find the missing part as he held on to his half. Tossing it aside, the search continued. The Tall Dark Man came across another scroll. It was about three battles. Reading it, he felt triumphant. The Dark Prophecy spoke of the third battle, which would raise demons and unleash a hell on earth that none, including the queen, could stop. He needed to bring back his stones, create the army of darkness and death, and here it was…the kicker to the queen that made him gloat. The Avenging Angel would be his redemption in the end, his bride and mother to all demons. Wait, did he read that right? He reread it. His bride. He couldn't kill her, but he could have his victory by making her his bride. This would undo the queen and her loyal supporters if he had the angel.

Chapter Three
Curses

Malakai, Seattle, Present Day

Malakai was distraught by the time Raven left him. He sulked for a time in his office before calling Marcus. He didn't want to alarm Amber or Chloe, but he hadn't felt himself since that woman came to him. Her breath lingered on him, and the words haunted his mind. "He will walk on all fours." That could only mean one thing. She cursed him to his wolf state, and he didn't know when that change would happen. There would be a full moon soon, and he was confident it would happen by then. Marcus would do his best to keep the girls safe.

He called Sabre. While he waited for Sabre to arrive, Malakai sat at his desk and penned a note to his love. He didn't want to hurt Amber, but her destiny had to come before his love for her. As he wrote the letter, a tear fell and smudged his words. His assistant knocked and showed Sabre into his office.

Malakai motioned to the chair before his desk and said, "Sabre, come sit. I need your help. A woman came by here today, and she said she serves him. The Tall Dark Man. And he's up to something if his wench is out of her cage."

"What the fuck? I thought he was gone into the pit." Sabre ran his hands through his hair and scratched his unshaven chin.

Malakai sighed and told him to sit down a second time. He did so.

Malakai continued, "This curse, well, isn't pleasant, that I can tell you. I've never experienced it, but I heard from others in my clan that this is a nightmare. Were any of the wolves cursed? It may be possible to break it. It depends on the curse and who cast it. Well, this Raven lady, I assume she's a witch. She came by here and insisted on seeing me. When I took her hand to greet her, she breathed in my ear and cursed me in a whisper so that only I would hear. I can't remember the exact words, but she was clear that a kiss from true love would not break the spell. I fear this spell will be the end of me. It sounded permanent and knowing…"

He couldn't finish before Sabre said, "Raven? Raven the Witch?"

"I believe so. Do you know this, Raven?"

Sabre scratched his head and shared his knowledge about Raven with Malakai.

"She's his all-powerful Dark Witch. She conducts dark magic, including necromancy, like no other witch." It gave Malakai the shivers just thinking about how powerful she must be to serve the Tall Dark Man. Sabre continued, "Legend says she is a Hexham witch. And not just any Hexham. Her ancestor is none other than Alison Hexham, daughter of Elizabeth Hexham. She absorbed all their powers, unlike the others. One of the dire wolves said once that she is the one who creates his demons while others bear his children. It's so twisted, but they say she never leaves his side. She's as powerful as our Chloe, if not more. If you say she came here, then I sense something sinister. Tell me more about what she whispered to you. It must be a clue or something."

Malakai tried to recall her curse, but all he remembered was that he would be trapped on all fours, meaning his wolf form. Amber could not break the curse. As Sabre listened, Malakai noticed he was taking his phone out of his pocket. He was going to make a call.

When Sabre made the call, Malakai could hear what he was saying. Then, Malakai noticed he had put the phone on speaker.

"This is Sabre. We must bring Malakai in for his safety. Soon, he will be on all fours, and we must keep him and the public safe while trying to break the curse. Let Black Wind know we are coming. Also, I informed the queen about the situation and told her I would protect Malakai with my life. We must hurry. Last, find anyone in the pack who knows about the Witch named Raven. We need everyone to help with this. Who knows what that Witch is doing?"

Malakai finished packing up his office and left a message with Human Resources that he had a personal family emergency and would require time off. He left detailed instructions for his assistant and receptionist. He believed the museum would be all right in his absence. He even checked Amber's and Chloe's offices, placing notes for them so that their assistants could fill in for their absences should they need to take leave. Since Amber worked nights, her assistant usually managed the day-to-day operations so she could prepare the exhibits while Chloe's schedule was flexible since most of the time she was studying the artifacts. Malakai still had to manage the museum and they all needed an income for the estate and other needs.

Once they reached his car, Malakai felt like something was watching them. He glanced over his shoulder but saw nothing. The hair stood on his arms, and he felt something was amiss. Sabre smelled the air and nudged him.

"I smell a demon," Sabre said, "but I can't see it. Get in, and let's go."

Malakai threw everything in the trunk and sat in the driver's seat, ready to flee. Sabre gave him directions to where they were going, but something followed them, and he sensed it.

***

Chloe, Seattle, Present Day

Chloe was waiting for Marcus to get up from his sleep. She couldn't wait to tell him about their discovery in the library. It was always so quiet when Marcus and Amber were sleeping in their coffins. Chloe spent about three days working to avoid the loneliness she felt. On the nights Marcus didn't need to feed, she cherished their time together. They were so much in love today as the day they first realized it was meant to be for them. It wasn't an easy adjustment at first but with the flexibility

Malakai gave her, it worked for them. She practiced her magic all the time because of her strong abilities. When she called upon her ancestor Sarah Good, she always learned that she was the witch discussed in the Witch's Prophecy. The all-powerful light witch would one day balance all the magic in the world with her daughter.

He was so weak when he returned but remained silent. It drove her crazy that he didn't want to tell her about what he had found. Since she was anxious, she entered her magic room and lit a candle in the center of the floor. She sat inside the pentagram drawn on the wooden floor and chanted. She called upon the ancient powers to guide her, to show her the way. Chloe hoped that the meditation would work.

A mist appeared, and a form stood in front of her. She didn't recognize the figure. It put its finger to its lips and motioned for her to be quiet. Chloe took it as a sign of something to aid in her journey. Before she knew it, another figure appeared next to the first one. She watched them in silence, hoping that she would understand their intention. The two figures moved towards her and began a chant. Chloe moved a little closer so that she could hear the whisperings.

"From ancient times to years
ahead, we call
upon the one who holds the
key.
Summon to me, summon to
thee.
Please bring me the essence,
the stone I seek.
Bring thee to me."

Chloe repeated the words so that she would memorize them. She wasn't sure what would happen if she repeated the words, but she would risk it all. Before Chloe could look up once more, the figures disappeared, and her candles lost their flames. She found her notebook and jotted down the words. Sensing the need to find Amber, Chloe was exhausted. She lay down for what she hoped would be a brief nap until Amber shook her awake.

"Chloe, wake up. I thought you were coming back to the library. Are you ok?"

"I think so. I just felt so tired, but I had this chant. The spirits gave it to me when I asked for guidance. Want to check it out?"

She tried to stand but got lightheaded, forcing her to sit down. Amber looked at her worriedly and said,

"Chloe, that's not like you; you almost lost your balance. What's wrong?"

Amber touched her forehead, but she could tell there were no signs Chloe was sick. Before she knew it, her hands shook. Her dark eyes rolled backward, and she spoke.

"Queen. I summon you to come to us. Sometimes she's old. Sometimes she's young, but she watches over the fires. She is one of the most powerful goddesses and holds the key you seek. Travel southwest till the mountains run into the sea, where the Kāne rules over all life, land, and sky. The Witch will guide you, but the angel hangs in the balance. Evil is no longer silent. Mark my words, queen. Days of peace will not exist if the stones are in the hands of evil and the angel's light becomes dark."

Chloe regained her senses and looked at Amber, who appeared somber as if she saw something that spooked her.

"Amber, you ok?"

Amber nodded, replying, "Chloe, what the fuck was that? Are you playing a trick on me or something? Who the hell is Kāne?"

Chloe looked perplexed, but a figure stood before them before she could utter a sound. She was translucent, and she was beautiful. The prophecy was in motion once more. Then the figure disappeared. Another wave of nausea overcame her and Chloe felt terrible again. As she shook nausea off, she thought for a moment. Then, like a lightbulb turning on for one of her discoveries, she laughed.

"Amber, Kāne is one god in Hawaii. He is the main god over all the gods. He is the one the Hawaiians refer to as their creator in their ancient ways. We have a few exhibits at the museum to educate the university students here. However, the exhibits will leave soon, and we have little time to investigate. They close less than one week. If I can touch them, I might see their past. It could give us a clue."

"Then let's get to the museum. I want to see them. One might help me with that riddle you told me five minutes ago. I thought we would have peace," said Amber, but not before continuing. "Zaraquel could be in danger if we don't succeed at whatever we are supposed to do. I'll drive, but you wake Marcus up now. The night is just beginning for us. I'll tell Jerome we are leaving and let him know what's going on."

Chloe nodded and went to wake up her husband.

***

The Tall Dark Man, Underground, Present Day

Occupying his throne, the Tall Dark Man let his thoughts of vengeance consume him every second. He kept thinking about the angel Zaraquel and how he would make her his bride. She was no longer a child who had to mind her parents, which pleased him immensely. She was a woman now. From the reports he received from Anne, she was succumbing further to the dark magic. If he planned to succeed, it would take time and patience. He reached out to Anne for another detailed update. Grabbing the crystal he used to communicate with the Witch, he summoned her. The Witch answered his call at once.

He asked, "Tell me, how is the little angel doing with her training? Have you taught her what I need her to know? Is she ready to become my wife?"

"Master, she is practicing the darkest of all magic now. Her wings, her light, it's all fading. It won't be much longer because she's hungry for knowledge, the power. It is consuming her. However, there is that annoying Nimue. She's going to have a bit of a problem. She keeps interfering, but I am not teaching her as intentionally as I am for the angel. I need more time before she gives in to darkness. I promise you, Master, she will be yours. All yours. You will have your avenging angel."

Rubbing his chin and adjusting the brim of his hat, he acknowledged her request and said that time is all hers if the angel becomes his.

***

Kūpa'aike'e, Hawaii Territory, the 1800s

Kūpa'aike'e was a proud Hawaiian, always respecting the gods of the land, sea, and sky. Together with his wife, Kalamau, the gods had already blessed them with seventeen children. Kalamau encouraged him, about once a week, to leave food for the goddess. In return, she blessed them with strong children, primarily boys. Kūpa, as he was known to his o'hana, was a strong warrior and chieftain. He was truly blessed to have served in many battles between the islands, for he never lost a battle.

It was a strange morning as he climbed the path to the volcano, the ancestral place of the fire goddess. Kalamau ensured the fish was cooked and wrapped in tea leaves, fruit, and poi for her. When he made it partway, he was stopped by a beautiful maiden with long black hair and skin so smooth, and her smile made him feel like a young Keiki kāne again, especially at his age.

"Aloha, Kūpa. Is that for me?"

"No, this is for the goddess Pele. In gratitude for the blessings my wife Kalamau and I have received, we never neglect our respect for the goddess. We have many children, and our name will live on. Some of my sons are blessed with warrior strength and agility to keep our islands safe. If you go to the village, seek my wife, and we will share our table with you."

The woman smiled at him, placing her hand on his shoulder, and said, "Kāne will keep you safe, and Kū will continue to give you strength to win the battles. But I, Goddess Pele, will protect your family from fire, lightning, or destruction. I accept your offering, and Kāne will once more bless you and your wife with another son. He will become a powerful kahuna. And one day, when he has fulfilled his destiny, he will become a kahuna nui—the most powerful sorcerer on the islands. When you name this son, you must name him Kamekona. If you don't, the gods will let you see their anger on your o'hana."

Kūpa, a man of honor of the islands and the gods, agreed to name his next son Kamekona. "Goddess Pele, you are most kind, and I thank you with my o'hana's love. My home will always be open to you and all other gods. You need not ask, just come to my home. Kalamau will be a loving friend to all who visit."

He handed her the offerings and bowed his head in great honor of the goddess before returning to his wife to tell her the joyous news. As he walked toward the village, he raised his head with pride. His ancestral family has been honored with his warrior abilities and a future son's destiny as a kahuna.

***

Raven, Seattle, Present Day

Raven stood outside the estate and watched from the bushes. She watched the comings and goings in the estate to plan. Raven noticed that the lights in the estate lit up inside when the night sky became darker. *This must mean they are home, and I had hoped for something else.* She kept watching and waiting.

She noticed two people leaving. It was them: the queen and her witch. Raven was disgusted and wouldn't even acknowledge their names under her breath. They were in a hurry, but the door opened again. It was Marcus, the witch's mate. Raven tilted her head and peered as she watched from the bushes. He was going with them. *This will be easy, then.* The estate would have to be empty. So, she took her chance.

She closed her eyes and called the Tall Dark Man to tell him where she was. Using telepathy, she told him of her plan that would allow her to astral project herself into the estate and look around. Then, she broke the connection before he could interject. This was her mission of service to complete her Master's favor.

Raven looked around again to ensure she wasn't discovered and closed her eyes again. She projected herself inside the estate and walked around. As soon as she saw the butler, she followed him a little. He walked past a library, so she ducked in there. Raven looked at the books and called upon her magic to move things around to see if she could find what she was after. Nothing. She continued upstairs. She looked inside all the rooms before feeling faint. Her power waned in this room. Then she saw it. A pentagram of power. This was the witch's room. She left and returned to her physical body once more.

Her mind called upon Arioch the Demon. She summoned him to her, and waited for him to show. One of the unique gifts that the Master always appreciated was their ability to teleport. Raven made sure that Arioch would have that ability and more to please him. The last thing she wanted was to disappoint the master.

"You summoned." Arioch was a massive-looking demon, one of her best creations for the Master. She watched him as he waited for her command.

Raven said, "Find Malakai, the wolf. When you do, bring him to the Master, and if anyone tries to stop you, kill them. Don't be afraid to leave a trail. They will not follow, and I will make sure of it."

Arioch bowed and left her. Raven smiled at the power she held. Since she rarely left the underground world, she seized the moment to rest and finish exploring the estate. Raven mused about finding another witch she could force into the hands of the Master. *If the Master needs more demons, he will need more powerful witches.* Raven wondered if she could call upon her ancestor, Elizabeth Hexham, from the other side.

***

Malakai, Seattle, Present Day

Malakai and Sabre were driving east of Seattle, heading towards the mountains. Malakai knew the dire wolves moved around to keep hidden when they wanted to run in their wolf form, so eastern Washington made the most sense. His hands trembled as he drove, and he tried to prevent Sabre from seeing them.

Sabre broke the silence. "Malakai, I've meant to ask you all this time. Whatever happened to your clan after you three left to save the baby? I try to watch for strays since wolves are rare now. One wolf found a pair of young ones living alone but didn't realize what they were. They didn't remember where they came from. We took them in and made them part of our pack."

He remained silent, but his mind thought fondly of his fallen friend Nikoli. He missed his friend but was happy that Miriam was reunited with them.

"I returned to Delaware, where the clan was, but it was too late. The wolves were slaughtered, and their skulls were placed on poles. I stayed for some time in the area, searching and hunting, but I couldn't find anyone I remembered. I feared I was alone. After a few months, I abandoned the camp we once called home and moved on to fulfill Nikoli's wish."

Malakai stopped abruptly as he realized he couldn't stop the tears. He was still a lost man, despite being an alpha. He loved his friend's daughter and wanted more with her. That was for another day. His troubles were beginning, or at least he thought. He hated the thought of being trapped as a wolf. Malakai even hated the idea of leaving Amber all alone.

"Sabre, can we fight against this Witch's curse? Do I have a chance?"

He noticed Sabre was silent, but then Sabre said, "Someone in the pack may know how to break the curse. It will not be easy. It will be like the days of the Blood Moon. Remember?" Laughing heartedly, Malakai felt a slight punch in his arm from his friend. It made him feel better. So, he kept driving, following the directions that Sabre gave him. Hopefully, it won't be much longer as the pain in his bones intensified and the tremors in his fingers to transform were distracting him from driving. He wasn't ready to lose his humanity. Not yet.

***

The Hawaiian Gods, Islands of Hawaii, Hawaiian Creation

The god Lono stood in front of his favorite heiau temple. He watched the many offerings of pigs, vegetables, and tapas laid by the young maidens, daughters of the island's farmers. He smiled at them, knowing he didn't make himself visible to them. But he saw her. The one wahine who captivated his heart amongst the Hawaiians. Her eyes showed him her passion for life and love. He knew Kāne would disapprove of the match. Though she was a farmer's daughter, her bloodline was pure and destined for greatness.

Lono knew he couldn't have her, but he could reward her for her beauty and the love of her o'hana. He disappeared into the trees and sat to carve a totem. Lono created a totem of life for her and left it under her mat that night. He loved the girl and talked to the other gods about her. Lono wanted her. Once he spoke to the others about her, they forbade him from having contact with her. The reason they gave was her destiny. Confused about her destiny, he began fighting with the others. Kāne said, "When a queen arrives equal to all, she will bring a young wahine whose wings will soar like the golden plover that brought these people to the islands for life and protection. Through your wahine that you hold affection for, her descendants will help the winged wahine to bring peace once more. A peace that Kū cannot stop. It will be a forbidden love."

Lono understood the other gods, his brothers, and vowed to guard the young wahine and her totem.

Chapter Four
Witchcraft

Raven, Seattle, Present Day

Raven found herself at a bar in downtown Seattle where she buried her weakness into her drink. She already knew her next step, and that was to find the book. She needed to get everyone in the estate out without causing suspicion. A man approached her and sat next to her. Mere human. He did not know that she was a powerful witch. She whispered a spell as he continued to flirt with her unsuccessfully, causing his hand to spill his drink all over himself. The bartender kicked the man out, thinking he was upsetting a customer. He apologized to Raven for the drunken man's behavior, but she just smiled and waved her hand in front of his face. Her powers were unstoppable. She made the bartender think she had paid for her drink when she didn't. The Master didn't provide her with any financial means, nor did she need it. She would find the book soon.

***

More potent than before, she approached the estate by the front entrance. She wasn't worried about the humans who protected this place. A man, the butler, answered the door and didn't recognize Raven. Raven thought this was all going according to her plan.

"Miss, I can't bid you entrance. There are no expected visitors at this hour. Would you like to leave your name?" The man was old but not feeble.

"Sir, I need entrance if you please. I'm an old friend of the late Michael. It's been a few years, but I knew Michael long ago. I heard he'd recently passed away."

The butler had no intention of letting her in, but she raised her palm towards her lips and blew into his face. A powdery substance entered his nostrils, and as he inhaled, he fell backward, unconscious. Raven called for the Master to send some of his lower-level demons to pick up the butler and hide him for her amusement later. The Master could never say no to her guilty pleasures.

Stepping over him, she found her way back to the library. She searched through the books and papers scattered there. Then, she noticed a handwritten page of notes or something. Raven couldn't read the handwriting but figured it must be important. Then she read a name. It was important. She pocketed the paper, continuing to rummage through the library. This was her game, the Master promised. She tore apart the library and, by doing so, she found the book. When Raven touched it, her hand burned and blistered. Taking a throw blanket from the sofa, she threw it on the book, but the blanket blew up in flames.

Raven had an idea.

"From your pages, unbind your
power.
Release the fire that burns
within.
Allow this dark Witch to take
control."

The book rattled, and the design on the cover turned yellow. A fire encompassed the book, and an unseen force sent Raven into the air and crashing against the wall. Now she was pissed. Stretching her hands outward and letting her eyes fixate on the book, she sent her power directly to the symbol. The book protected itself. Then she looked closer at the symbol. Cursing, she realized she was the fool. The book was not an ordinary book that the Master sent her after. The symbol was a powerful deterrent against evil. It was the ancient book of the prophecy. It was going to be complicated. She left the estate to return later. The Witch might be the key if Raven could capture her. She refused to fail the Master, or it might cost her dearly.

As she walked the streets, she found a dark alley and sat in a corner. Closing her eyes, she breathed in deeply and summoned a connection to the Tall Dark Man.

"Fama."

In her mind, she listened to his words before she returned any answers.

"Master, about the book. It's well protected, and I must capture the Witch Chloe to break it. Only she equals my power to break such a protection spell. I need a demon to fetch the bitch and bring her to me. Will you send me a demon, great Master?"

She could hear the Tall Dark Man laughing at the request. She was fuming if he thought to taunt her. Then he replied.

"I will do better than send you a demon. Do you know my little plan to capture the avenging angel? I will have the Witch Anne teach the angel how to create a demon that will covet the book for me. You have pleased me, Raven. You remind me so much of my Elizabeth. Leave the witch alone for now. I want her to see the fall of the angel. And I have other plans for her. Closer to the heart plans. In the meantime, find Arioch and bring me the werewolf."

Raven smiled. "It will be done, master."

***

Zaraquel, Witch's Cottage, Present Day

Drained of emotion and feelings, Zaraquel sought Anne, the Witch. Day after day, Zaraquel kept practicing the spells. She could feel herself mastering the spells but kept a close watch on the color of her wings. However, today was different. Anne was excited about something that did not fit her usual behavior, making Zaraquel uneasy.

"Anne, why are you so excited? Is it because I'm mastering all the spells and becoming your best student?"

Zaraquel tried to sound like an innocent student, but something inside her told her to be careful. Then she heard Nimue's voice once more in her head. Nimue's message kept playing in her mind like a song on repeat. Anne reached for her hand, and Zaraquel let her hold it. She could feel the cold skin but thought nothing of it. Finally, Anne spoke.

"Angel, there is an important spell only some witches can learn. I've been asked to show you the darkest of spells, and while this one may not be that dark, it will make you one of the most powerful witches. More powerful than your mother. Would you like to learn, child?"

Feeling uneasy, Zaraquel knew she had to master all the light and dark magic spells, she nodded while looking at her feet. She didn't want to hear the comparison of her power to her mother's because she knew that her mother was the most powerful witch in the world. Shuffling her feet back and forth, Zaraquel summoned the courage and looked the Witch dead in the eye, saying, "I want to learn anything you will teach me. I was just, um, missing my family. I know what my father said to you so that you would teach me. Do you know how long I must stay here?"

Anne placed her cold hand on Zaraquel's cheek, sending shivers up her spine. Zaraquel ignored the feeling and tried to look like a willing student. Ultimately, she didn't think Anne had bought it because the cold hand turned into a slap against Zaraquel's cheek with a stern warning.

"Powerful angels who are witches of both light and dark magic cannot show favor to emotions. Time for the next lesson. We will create a demon of your choosing, and I will teach you as you create your demon. Only you can control your demon."

Zaraquel took this chance to poke at Anne a little further. She realized Anne hated Nimue and thought, *Now's the time*. Before speaking to Anne, she watched the Witch's moves more closely. The Witch hustled about the kitchen preparing ingredients for the upcoming lesson, and Zaraquel inspected some ingredients. *Hmm*, she thought. *The witch is using things Uncle Mac said should never be used under any circumstances. Light or dark magic. So, what does she want me to do?*

"Anne, I'm curious. The new spell you want to teach me. When do witches use this kind of spell? I never thought demons were created. I thought they were just born like the rest of us."

"Oh, Angel, you are a delight! Some demons are born, yes. But when you need a demon for strength to control and do your bidding, you need to create them from magic. I never really thought of it more than that. There are other spells you need to learn, too. Time is on our side unless you want to stop learning and go home. If you do that, I will let you go. Still, I will erase all your memories of the spells I taught you. If I remember correctly, you have a specific purpose for learning dark magic. Isn't that right, my sweet?"

"I don't want to leave. At least not yet. I am still your student. It's just… well… Uncle Mac only taught me one type of magic, but the world holds so much more. I don't want to disappoint you, Anne, and I am ready to learn."

Anne smiled at Zaraquel and showed her teeth a little more than usual. She noticed the witch was beautiful, but her eyes always hid something. Zaraquel could sense that, and her senses never betrayed her. She cautiously looked at her wings once more. They were still not red, which allowed her to keep fooling the Witch until Nimue returned with help. At least, that's what she kept telling herself.

***

The Tall Dark Man, Underground, Present Day

The Tall Dark Man decided it was time to play with his sweet Mary. Calling her to his chambers, he waited for her to approach. Mary was a timid thing ever since she became his. She always did as he bid because he promised no harm would ever come to her husband. But since his demise, he had already informed Mary that leaving was never an option. She had the power of immortality over the centuries in his lair, and he ensured that her beauty never faded. She stood in the doorway, as always, until he called for her to come closer. The Tall Dark Man wanted to savor her beauty as he eyed her up and down. The once beautiful blue dress was tattered and faded from time. His crooked finger motioned to come closer.

"Master, you called for me. Are you going to set me free? A change of heart, Master?"

He shuddered at the thought of someone thinking he had a heart. That little word irritated him, and he made Mary kneel before him. He looked at the tears that fell down her cheeks, and her defiance only made him more sinister. Using a finger under her chin, he tilted her face upward so she would be forced to look at him.

"Sweet, sweet Mary. In that little brain of yours are secrets from that night. Do you remember that night? You and your precious son were drained of life, left on the earth until one of my witches found you. Here's the kicker. There was still enough in you to bring you back. You were not completely dead. I willed you back to life as insurance for Valentine's compliance. Now here you are with me. And all I asked was your obedience while your husband, my Hunter, roamed the world, killing those who stood in my way. Now, with him dead, you can be useful to me or useless. Choose now, sweet Mary, and I may give you a present that would only make you reconsider your affection."

He watched her face as she stared into his eyes. He held onto her chin tightly to show her his true intentions. The Tall Dark Man relished in the fear in her eyes. Deep down, he knew what her choice would be. He knew she never wanted to die, even when the witches brought her to him all those years ago. She begged for her life, much to his delight.

Mary finally said, "I choose you, Master. You know I will always choose you. Valentine could've come back for me, but he chose not to. And why? Because he chose you. Just like I chose you. You let me learn from your witches. I roam your home all these centuries, but for what? For me to choose you? I always choose you, and you have never given me a present. Till now. Why?"

She spat at his feet, defiant looking as ever. He loved when she showed these spurts of strength and became complacent again. The Tall Dark Man confused her and played with her some more. He closed his eyes and sent a command to one of his witches. She entered the room a few minutes later with a baby in her arms. He turned Mary's face to look at the witch with the baby in her arms. Then a sign of recognition came across her face. The Tall Dark Man realized Mary recognized the babe.

"Is that…that my baby? Is it Elijah?"

The Tall Dark Man snickered as he released Mary. He stood and motioned for the witch to bring the baby. The Tall Dark Man showed no emotion as Mary ran to her baby and took him from the Witch. Watching her with the baby, he dominated her once more. To seal the deal. Nodding to the witch, the witch took back the baby, and he cried. Mary screamed. Turning towards him, she screamed again.

"Give me my baby! My Elijah!"

"You can have him back on one condition, my sweet Mary. Are you listening to me, sweet Mary?"

Mary nodded. He spoke again, this time with a vengeance in his heart.

"I need you to go out above, find and become best friends with the witch Chloe. Separate her from the queen. My witches will see that your powers grow. This way, Chloe will not be wary of such a new person. One of my witches will accompany you, and you will remain above until your assignment is complete."

"But I'll be separated again from my baby, so I'm no better off choosing to serve you or not. Either way, you keep me away from my baby."

"I'll sweeten the deal for you, my lovely Mary. You can take your baby with you, and when you are with the witch Chloe, your baby will be with the witch I sent you above. This way, you will serve me and have your baby. All to guarantee your service."

Mary didn't take long before answering yes. The Tall Dark Man was satisfied and told the witch to begin preparations in training Mary once she had an hour with her baby first. His brilliant mind was working in full force, and while his Mary was learning witchcraft, he allowed his mind to continue thinking about the scroll he found. His plan to gain control of the angel was working perfectly–with just one slight change. Instead of keeping her like the other witches,

he was to marry the avenging angel. This would weaken
the queen!

***

Anne Koldings, Denmark, July 1590

Imprisoned in Copenhagen, Anne sat in her cell
with several others accused of witchcraft and another
action against the Princess of Denmark. Anne was
believed to be part of a group that summoned the storms
that would prevent James VI from collecting his bride.
Princess Anna, daughter of Frederick II, was betrothed to
him. While she faced her accusers, Anne snorted at the
men who spat and ridiculed her. At least in her cell, she
was with those that faced the same accusations and the
relentless bantering. The others finally fell asleep as
silence filled the cell.

Anne couldn't sleep as she watched the rats scurry
between the others. Hands would slap at the rats, trying
to chase them away. A rat approached her feet, and she
just stared at it. The rat twitched its nose and then
changed. A man stood before her with the same dark
eyes as the rat. The hair stood on her arms as she saw
this transformation.

He said, "My sweet little Witch. You find yourself in quite a predicament, don't you?"

"Master. I have not broken my sworn fealty to you. They know nothing of you."

Her Master lowered the brim of his hat, shielding his eyes as he waited for her to make her next move. Anne couldn't decide what else he could want from her. She swore her fealty to him and collaborated with the other witches that caused the storms to appear when the Princess of Denmark was out to sea with her intended husband. Something about that marriage kept him on edge. He was insistent about her casting certain spells about the storms. Then he spoke.

"The princess survived, as well as James VI. I wanted them lost at sea. Your storms were not powerful. Why? I gave you an immense amount of power in the craft."

"Master, others were involved, and one broke the circle, weakening the storm. Is there another way I can serve you?"

She noticed the Master looked lost in thought before giving her a command.

"I know they call you the mother of the devil, yet you never conceived. Let's make the name they gave you true."

"How do you know what the men of this land call me since my trial?"

"Sweet child. I know everything that my witches go through. It's part of my charm. I love all the witches that serve me faithfully. Anne, you will become the mother of the devil. You will bear my demons for eternity, never growing old. And I will reward you with a special gift of mine. You will become another powerful witch, yet your power will not diminish with the bearing of my demons. Will you give your loyalty to me again?"

"Yes, Master. But I am sentenced to die. I could tell based on the trial, and I confessed my craft but not of my loyalty to you."

"Take a strand of your hair and place it on this stone," he said as he handed her the odd-shaped stone. "Then close your eyes, wish the stone to take in your likeness, and blow life into it from your breath."

Anne did as she was bid, staring at her identical self before she could blink twice. The eyes were a solid black, showing no pupil or even blinking. She motioned for the stone image of herself to lie on the cot she occupied, and she and her Master disappeared into the night.

The next thing Anne knew, she was in her little cottage in a dark forest, away from sunlight and others.

The Master wasted no time ensuring she kept her part of the oath as he laid her down on the earth and ravaged her body. He explored every inch of her body with his fingers, tongue, and breath. She closed her eyes, wondering if this was what it would be like each time. Anne knew his evil nature, and it carried through in his passion for her. Somehow, he ensured she would obey him without fault if he made her succumb to her primal side in their lovemaking. He was gentle enough to make her body beg for more but rough to keep her wanting more of him. He wanted to make sure she birthed the demons that would be in his likeness. Her body tingled at his touch, and she spread her legs wider to take more of him in.

"Master. I will birth your demons if you take me like this each time. There will even be two demons at a time, occasionally. I am yours. Take me. Fill me."

Anne groaned more as he penetrated deeper inside her body. When he finished, he kissed her hands and said, "Birth, my demons, witch. You will have power and beauty, and I will return for my them. And then we will begin again."

She laid back as she watched him disappear, leaving her alone in the cottage. She placed a hand on her belly and sensed his seed taking hold.

***

Chloe, Seattle Museum, Present Day

Chloe and Amber unlocked the doors to the employee's entrance and found their way to their offices. Marcus trailed behind them until he stopped.

"Amber, smell that?"

Chloe turned around and looked at Amber and Marcus. She saw Amber sniffing the room. Her nose twitched as if she smelled something horrible.

Trying to smell, Chloe said, "What is it? Remember, I'm a witch, and my nose doesn't pick up smells like yours, honey; it's a dark witch. A dark witch was here. Malakai was here. I don't want to alarm you both, but I received a call from Malakai earlier. He called me because he may need my coven's help. Sabre has him. The dark witch. She smells of the Tall Dark Man. Malakai thinks she did something to him, and Sabre will help him. My job is to keep you both safe and ensure our daughter's safety because she used a powerful curse against him. Something that even you, Amber, can't undo with a kiss. We are up against this dark magic if we try to save Malakai, which we need to do. I asked my coven to gather as much information on this dark witch as we can. We aren't even sure my power is a match for hers."

Chloe heard a sound coming from one hallway. Putting her finger to her lips, she hushed Marcus and Amber. Chloe took her hands and weaved them in a circle. She whispered the word *Quaerite*. In her palms, a red ball appeared, and she hurled it down the hallway. Considering the closed museum, the red ball would find what made the noise. Chloe realized the light was illuminating the hallway, and she followed it. Amber and Marcus followed her.

As she followed the light down the hallway, Marcus spoke. "It's not the witch I smell, but something else. It also smells of The Tall Dark Man. He found a way back after the battle. But right now we need to know what's in here with us."

As they turned left, Chloe realized this hallway had a closet at the end. She worked her magic again, following the red ball down the hall. She screamed. In front of her stood a stone demon. Chloe wondered how long he was waiting by the door for her. She couldn't tell if he was real or just a spook. He was large and reached for her. He was real! She felt his hand brush lightly against her cheek with his long arms. As she eyed his size, she realized he was over six feet tall. Marcus and Amber leaped in the air and landed before the demon, keeping Chloe safe. Amber lunged for the demon's arm while Marcus tried for the head. Chloe moved three steps forward and chanted.

"Demon of stone, a demon
from hell.
Crumble to the earth upon
my spell."

To her dismay, nothing happened to the stone demon. She saw Amber and Marcus struggling to keep hold of him. The demon pulled his arm back and flung amber away, but she landed on all fours. He shook his other arm, sending Marcus against the wall. Chloe saw both vampires looking fierce and full of rage. The demon looked at Chloe and said, "Wolf. Master wants."

Chloe dodged his attempts at capturing her and ran around the room. She tried to get behind Marcus, but the demon shot flames from his hands.

Moving out of the way to avoid being burned, Chloe yelled, "What the fuck was that? Marcus! The demon has magic?"

Marcus tried to stand before her, but the stone demon sent flames in his direction. His coat burned. Chloe saw he was tearing at it to remove it, and Amber stood facing

Chloe. Her birthmark glowed, and she knew Amber was in full power now. Amber touched the crystal around her neck and said, "Serve me, demon. I am the queen of all supernatural creatures. Disobey me and die."

The demon laughed. Chloe then saw that they were not any match for this stone demon. He taunted the queen, and Marcus was no match for him. Chloe feared what would happen next.

"What do you want, demon? You are not Krieg."

The demon laughed again. "Wolf. Master wants."

That's when Chloe realized that the Tall Dark Man wanted Malakai, and she screamed and used all her light magic to stop him.

"I call the spirits of my ancestors to give me strength."

Chloe closed her eyes, and a white owl stood next to her. The owl flew from her and started poking at the eyes of the demon. The demon screamed but did not go down. Instead, the owl fell to the ground with one arm movement from the demon. Chloe opened her eyes and took a deep breath.

"*Silentio*." The room stilled, and only Chloe and the demon could move. Chloe looked at Amber and Marcus, who were frozen in their places.

"Demon," Chloe said, "you must have a name. What is it?"

The demon looked at her with wonder and didn't answer.

Chloe chanted, "*Impero tibi. Nomen tuum.*"

"Demon name. Arioch. Master wants the wolf."

Chloe tried to keep calm, though she was terrified. Malakai. Amber's love.

"Arioch. I'm Chloe. Will you talk with me?"

While she did her best to make small talk with Arioch, she placed one hand behind her back and undid the spell that kept Marcus and Amber frozen. She hoped that neither would scare Arioch and that something would happen to her. From the corner of her eye, she noticed Marcus motioning slowly for Amber to hint at her plan. She counted on the intense training she and Marcus had always done together for him to know her thoughts. Arioch still spoke in choppy sentences but had the mind of a toddler. Chloe used this to her advantage.

"Friend. Arioch and Chloe are friends. Yes?"

Arioch said, "Master wants a wolf. What is a friend?"

Chloe upped her game a little. "I'm going to sing Arioch a song. Just close your eyes and listen. Ok, Arioch?"

The demon nodded, reminding her he was childlike.

Using her mother-like voice, she sang him with a spell that allowed him only to see her. He wouldn't see Marcus and Amber slowly passing the demon. Once she saw them disappear towards one office, Chloe cast a spell on Arioch, sending him back to where he came from. She didn't know exactly from where, but she sent him back to his Master. Drained from the spell, she collapsed on the ground, and when she came to, Marcus was cradling her.

Chloe looked up and said, "My love. He was too powerful for me and a demon who served the Tall Dark Man. We must look at the artifacts, but I need to rest first. You and Amber need to look. Let me rest in my office. My love…" Her voice trailed off as she fell asleep.

Chapter Five
Consequences

McPherson, Dark Forest, Present Day

McPherson, Rowe, Kabos, and Nimue wandered through the forest searching for the Totem of Life. With the Totem of Death wrapped in a cloth, McPherson walked carefully, fully aware of him carrying the item. As the four walked on a path that showed itself to Rowe, McPherson kept asking Nimue about Zaraquel. He was worried about that angel. Marcus and Chloe appointed him her guardian if anything happened to them, so he considered her a daughter.

Marcus said, "Nimue, tell us more about the witch. She's a dark witch but tells us about her power. What did you notice?"

Nimue was silent as she looked at the ground. McPherson noticed she was perhaps quiet because of her past. He took this opportunity to reassure her. Placing a hand around her, he pulled her close and held her tight. Nimue broke the silence with what seemed like a long-overdue cry of pain. McPherson understood she needed time before speaking to them about what the girls must've endured. Finally, after a deep cry, she told them all.

"The Witch is always talking to someone who isn't there. I think she's relaying messages to him. We shouldn't have gone with her, McPherson. I'm so sorry I didn't bring Z with me. I had to leave her, but I didn't want to, but… Merlin needed me."

McPherson asked, "Who is the witch talking to, Nimue?"

"The Tall Dark Man. Him. He's back. The Witch plans to hand Z over to him. McPherson, we must stop the Witch. She's mighty and has all these herbs and potions. Mandrake root, too. Lots of it. What does he want with Z?" Nimue couldn't stop sobbing.

McPherson just held her close and promised her they would save her. Then Nimue told them how Marcus promised Z would learn what she needed. Once McPherson heard Marcus would surrender to the Tall Dark Man, he regretted leaving the girls with that Witch. *Fuck*, he thought. *Can this get any worse?*

Turning to face Kabos and Rowe, McPherson tried to look at them for guidance. Kabos spoke first.

"The Tall Dark Man must never get his hands on the book Michael had before his death. That book belongs to the Romani clan. My clan. It holds the key to the prophecy but will only reveal itself to a just keeper. The book is older than me and holds the story of blood and dark prophecies. Yes, there are two prophecies, not just one. There is a story of two siblings of the prophecy. We must get to the queen and the book. So, let's find this other totem. And quickly."

Shocked at what he had just heard, McPherson could barely stand. Two prophecies? A dark one? *Holy Shit. Amber and Chloe, I need to get back to them and Zaraquel.* His mind was racing, and he could feel his blood pressure rising alarmingly. Rowe looked at him as if he could sense his thinking and said, "My boy, relax. The Tall Dark Man will always be a threat to the queen. But if you have been training her, Zaraquel and the others will be his threat. Not the other way around. Let's concentrate on the totem we are searching for. And then we can rescue Zaraquel from the dark Witch. You don't want to hear these words, but Zaraquel must learn the dark magic and the light to become one. Nimue, my dear, where do we go now?"

He felt calmer once Rowe finished speaking, and they followed Nimue as she led the way.

***

Malakai, Eastern Washington, Present Day

Malakai and Sabre reached the home of the dire wolves after four hours of driving east on I-90. Malakai could sense the change in the air as the mountains called to his instincts. As Sabre removed the bags from the trunk and led the way, he breathed in that sweet mountain air. His mind returned to the mountains of Delaware when he was with Nikoli and Miriam. As Malakai relished the thought, a pain seized him from his insides and dropped him to the ground like a stone. He screamed, "Sabre! Something's happening… God, it hurts…"

His words trailed off, only to be replaced with a howl.

Sabre screamed for the wolves. "Black Wind! Light Foot! Come help us now!"

Malakai's body burned as he stayed on all fours, though he was still human. He could hear Raven's voice in his head, whispering the curse over repeatedly, as fingers became longer, as nails grew, and he screamed. Through his screams, he could hear other voices. He figured it must have been Black Wind and Light Feet! He remembered Sabre calling for them. Malakai tried to speak, but it wasn't easy. He took a few breaths and used his remaining strength to say what he needed to say quickly.

"Sabre. The change and her curse are working. Save me, my friend."

Sabre brought Black Wind closer to Malakai. Black Wind kneeled on the ground, saying, "Brother, don't talk. We will fix this curse, but you must change before the curse changes you. There is no time to wait. Look, the change is happening already. I can't answer how long you will be a wolf, but you must stay calm. The hard part is not to hunt. Resist animal behavior for us to break the curse. If you surrender to being an animal, there is no chance for you to become human again. We will break this witch Raven's curse. I swear to you, brother. I swear."

Malakai nodded, tears running down his cheeks as he only thought of Amber. He screamed again and followed with a howl. His eyes watched as his nails grew, the hair on his arms grew thicker, and his bones cracked. Malakai looked again up to Sabre and said, "Save me." Those were his last human words as he willed the change on his terms, shedding his human form.

Sabre wrapped his arms around his neck and rested his head against Malakai's fur.

"I give you my word, brother wolf and friend. I will break this bitch's curse."

***

Raven, Seattle, Present Day

Raven wandered the streets searching for Arioch. Once she realized Arioch was not heeding her command to return to her, Raven became frustrated. Using a powerful force that would've brought the buildings down, she was sure that Arioch would respond, and he didn't. Raven had to think for a moment.

"Praecipio tibi venire."

Raven waited and then repeated the words in a more demanding voice. She hoped her summons would get through his thick stone skull and he would obey. The book would stay there until the Master sent a demon to assist her. Bringing the werewolf back would please him in the interim. However, she needed help to reach Arioch. After waiting long enough for any response, she returned to the Master to tell him that Arioch was not responding to commands and would await her punishment for failure. This would go poorly.

Raven sauntered through the halls of the underground and approached the throne room. The Master was in his chair, and in front of him stood Arioch. Rapping his knuckles against the side of the chair, she could see that he was in a foul mood, but he always was.

Aware of what might happen, Raven said, "Master. I summoned Arioch, but he has yet to respond to my calls. But pardon my naivety; I see he is with you."

"I thought I told you to take Arioch and bring me the wolf. How hard can that be?"

Raven promised herself not to fear his wrath, yet she still did.

"It isn't hard," she said. "I don't understand how Arioch didn't respond to my summoning. We can leave at once to search for the wolf. I promise you, Master, we will not return until the wolf is in chains. My curse should work its way to changing him so he can't alert the queen. He will be easy to find, as he will be an animal." She giggled at the thought and then returned to seriousness.

The Master looked pleased. His fingers stroked his chin while he was lost in thought. Arioch remained still, waiting for orders. The Tall Dark Man broke the silence in the room.

"Raven, Arioch, find and bring me the wolf. Arioch, I will crumble you if you do not heed Raven's commands. You are to obey her."

Arioch turned and said, "Witch and Arioch are friends. She sent me home to Master."

The Tall Dark Man grew angrier at the news. Baring his palm towards Raven and Arioch, fire shot through his hands and tore into Raven's body. She screamed. Once she stood again, she used a spell to heal herself and said, "What Witch? I command you to tell the Master everything using my voice."

Arioch nodded and looked into Raven's eyes. Raven could feel his connection, and then she spoke his words.

"I found Witch and Queen. Arioch is strong against the queen and vampire. But Witch was too powerful. Witch and Arioch are friends, and she sang a song, and then Arioch is here."

Raven broke the connection and realized that the witch was as strong as she was to subdue Arioch like this. She said, "Master. It's the witch Chloe. She broke through my spell, but it cost her all her energy. I must place another spell on Arioch before we can search for the wolf."

The Tall Dark Man nodded, and she toughened her control on the demon, but it still wasn't enough. He was getting impatient with her; she could tell by his stare. With a flick of his wrist, another witch unexpectedly stood beside him. Extending his hand toward her, she took it. As the witch approached, Raven recognized the familial features she had seen in several pictures of her family. It was her family matriarch. Elizabeth Hexham. Raven could only bow in reverence to the incredible power her matriarch held.

The Tall Dark Man told Elizabeth, "I need you to command my demon to obey Raven so the wolf will be mine. Do this, my Witch."

Elizabeth started arguing with him about the pit and leaving her to die, and the Tall Dark Man silenced her protests with a slap across the face.

"I made you," he said. "Therefore, I can break you. That will end your family line if you disobey me, witch. And to think, you were my favorite witch in my all-powerful Hexham coven. With your death, sweet Elizabeth, your descendant Raven will be no more. That choice is yours."

Raven tried not to show fear in her eyes. Still, she connected with Elizabeth Hexham and saw that her matriarch would obey him. She felt power coursing through her veins as she had never felt before.

Elizabeth said, "Raven, perform your spell on the demon as the master requests. You now have my power amplified through your veins. Master, I need to rest to regain full power to serve you better. May I have your permission?"

The Tall Dark Man nodded, kissed her hand, and took her to his bedchamber. Raven knew the signs all too well. She strengthened her control over Arioch before they left to search for the wolf.

***

The Tall Dark Man, France, 1559

The Tall Dark Man, disguised as a young boy, sat in the back of the court, watching and waiting. He saw his servant Nostradamus seated near the Queen Consort Catherine de Medici and Henry, King of France. *Nostradamus kept his promise, and he was loyal.* The King and Queen were hearing members of the court air grievances, and Henry broke the monotony of the quibbles that came before him.

"Let's hear from the court's prophet. Enlighten us, Nostradamus, with one of your prophecies.

Nostradamus moved from the side to the front of the court to face all. Queen Catherine sat on her throne, mesmerized by her prophet, until she saw the boy. Recognition of his image crossed her face as she interrupted the court with an order. "Boy, you - back there. Come forward to me. I remember you."

The Tall Dark Man made his way forward and bowed to the queen. The King asked her how she knew the boy, and that's when her loyalty to him proved more decisive than her marriage. The queen didn't shift uneasily but said, "When I was young, his mother and I were friends. I met him when she introduced me not that long ago, before her death. You were indisposed with one of your briefings, and I could not introduce you, husband."

Her lie satisfied the King, and he ushered the boy closer. The Tall Dark Man, still in disguise, made his way up to the King and queen. *Things are going according to the plan*, he thought.

"Nostradamus," said the king, "have you need of a young boy to help you in your service to the crown? We can't let the queen's friend's orphan go without a proper home. Would you like that, boy? To live in court with us?"

He took this time to nod yes, as it gave way to his plan to meet with Nostradamus for the next part of his plan. He was determined to find the prophecy and its keepers and knew Nostradamus would have an idea. The Tall Dark Man was ushered to Nostradamus, and the two were reunited. Nostradamus also recognized his disguise and was friendly as he said, "Sire, should I share my prophecy with you as you requested?"

"Yes, please. We need to hear this."

Nostradamus cleared his throat and said, "The young lion will overcome the older one on the battlefield in single combat. He will pierce his eyes through a golden cage. Two wounds become one, and he dies a cruel death."

The Tall Dark Man smiled as he knew Nostradamus was very gifted. Nostradamus recused himself to prepare his new servant, which only delighted the Tall Dark Man. He needed to speak to Nostradamus as soon as possible. Once they were alone, the Tall Dark Man transformed into the man Nostradamus was familiar with. Quickly, he drew the draperies to prevent anyone from seeing them.

The Tall Dark Man shifted in his place and asked Nostradamus to sit as he said, "While you serve the queen, certain things are in motion. You already shared your vision of the King's impending death. Only a fool would not take heed of that. I need you to see it. And a most particular act that would let you treat the son. Poison him, make him ill. I don't care. But the King's son must fall, causing a rift between the two women: Catherine de Medici and the young Mary. Young Mary must never rule alone over France. Catherine must rule over France either as regent or on her own. My sweet Catherine will be rewarded with immense powers, and you will gain more visions that will make you legendary past your mortal death. Unless you want something else, dear Nostradamus? Young Mary must be forced to leave France as I have other intentions for her."

"No, Master. I will be honored with the visions. I know of certain powders that can be used. Since my arrival here at court, I have learned that Catherine is quite the lady in power. She is most deserving of your rewards. I am indebted to you, Master."

He walked around the room a bit, studying the tools that Catherine had bestowed upon Nostradamus. He smiled as he touched the different pouches of powders, books, and even jewels. The Tall Dark Man was beyond pleased that Nostradamus entered into his alliance but then again, he knew that he would never have passed up an opportunity regarding his prophecies.

Turning to Nostradamus, he asked him about his time in Catherine's presence because her reports to him felt like something was off according to his plan.

"Master, I am confident I will see the King's death in under six months. Catherine was told of this so she may continue serving you as required. However, the young prince will come to the throne and secure the line. The young Mary is the only thing that makes me cautious about the line. My visions show the young Mary and Catherine battling for the throne and reign of the country but not much more than that. Perhaps time. As your servant, is there anything you can do to help me see past this?"

The Tall Dark Man paced and saw a small stone near a vase in the corner of the room. He picked up the stone and looked at it with intensity, looked at it intensely, and smiled. His powers were no match for anyone in this court. He knew what to do.

"Take this stone after I place a spell on it. When I leave your sight, the stone will transform. It will be in the boy's image. He will not speak but will obey your commands. The King will not be the wiser. The stone boy will crumble upon the King's death, as his usefulness will no longer be needed."

He noticed that Nostradamus held his breath in anticipation. Holding the stone up so that he and Nostradamus could see it fully, he began to whisper the words of transformation. The stone, originally grey in color, looked like any other stone that one could find when walking in the garden and turned a deep black. Any ragged, rough edges were immediately transformed into smooth sides. The Tall Dark Man held out the stone for Nostradamus to take.

"Remember what I said. The stone will transform once I leave. He is to be the boy – an exact image of what the court saw a while ago. He will not speak but obey your commands. In fact, through the stone boy, you can speak to him of your reports and I will receive them. You may only let Catherine know of the deception to take place. Continue to serve me, Nostradamus. In the end, the rewards you will have will be great."

Nostradamus smiled and took the stone. With a nod, he said, "I will serve you for all time, master."

With that, the Tall Dark Man vanished.

Chapter Six
All Over Again

Kawika (David) Kekahuna, Honolulu, Present Day

Kawika Kekahuna has served as the Chief Curator of one of Hawaii's most famous museums, celebrating the ancient history of the Hawaiian people for decades. Kawika and his team prepared the museum for a month-long exhibition to honor the Hawaiian gods. His team reported that the relics displayed signs of belonging to the god Kū and Kāne. He read through the latest report and put down his glasses. Kawika was sure that what he wrote was a prank by some interns studying the exhibit relics. He felt a pull toward the bookshelf, where the ancient texts of Hawaiian history were kept for research.

Climbing the ladder, he searched for the top row of the oldest books. Kawika couldn't explain how he knew where to look, but an image appeared as his fingers touched the texts: a group of koa fighting against the loko' ino. The loko' ino, evil spirits, were demons: the Kaimoni. The images disturbed Kawika so much that he fell off the ladder.

One of his interns rushed from the other side of the room and kneeled beside him. Cradling his head in her lap, Kawika was unaware of his actions. With his eyes still closed, he raised his hand and said, "The Kaimoni are coming. Evil will be unleashed on the lands of Hawaii. The land and our people are not safe till the koa come. The koa is not Hawaiian but is royalty in her own right."

The intern tried to hush him, but Kawika did not have it. He struggled to stand but managed with the intern's help.

He said, "I don't know what came over me, Malia. My sincere apologies. I must've dreamed this vision."

"Mr. Kekahuna, my tūtū always says to trust the visions. They are gifts from the gods."

"Ah, Malia. You are right. It's just that few Hawaiians remain that honor the ancient ways. It's one reason I brought you on board."

He regained all his faculties, and as he sat down, Malia brought him the relic she was studying. Holding it, he turned it around to see its magnificent woodwork.

Kawika asked, "Have you dated this piece?"

"I haven't been able to. The wood belongs to the koa tree. I could determine that, but not the age of the relic. When I hold it, I feel strange, however. Lightheaded."

Kawika studied the relic and motioned up at the ancient texts. Malia understood and fetched a handful of the texts from the shelf. As she handed him the texts, he started thumbing through the pages, and in the fourth book, he found a sketch that looked remarkably close to the relic. His thumb followed the lines of text, and he read. He summarized as he said out loud, "Malia, it says here that the idol is believed to have been made by the god Kū himself. The relic was lost at one point, never to be found again. The Kahuna Anaana had kept this relic under their watch until it was lost. It was assumed that the relic was lost before the colonization of Hawaii by outsiders. That's from this book. Let's see about the others."

Kawika and Malia found other sources that provided more detail about the relic, including how Kū may have transformed one of the island's most potent kahunas into the relic as punishment for not honoring the god. Kawika recalled that legend from childhood, but the details eluded his thoughts as he felt another vision coming. He kept this family trait, his gift of sight, hidden from everyone.

"Mr. Kekahuna, are you with me?"

Hearing Malia's voice brought him out of the trance, but he had to tell someone about what he saw. He told Malia more about the Kaimoni and a ghastly battle that would come to the islands. The look in her eyes said it all. They were in danger.

***

Zaraquel, Witch's Cottage, Present Day

Zaraquel started daydreaming as the witch Anne was speaking to her. She couldn't take the witch's voice or the constant demands about doing this or that. Zaraquel missed her mother and father with fierce emotion. The witch was silent but called for her attention.

"Now, make your demon with the ingredients I lay before you on the table."

Zaraquel studied the ingredients and eyed the mandrake root. There were so many that Uncle Mac had forbidden, but her curiosity got the best of her. She picked up each ingredient and took a close look at them. Turning them over in her hands, she memorized their characteristics. Since she ignored the lecture from the witch, Zaraquel wasn't sure what to do next. The witch must have noticed her stalling.

"Angel, pay attention. Mix the ingredients in the cauldron—all but the mandrake root. Don't breathe in the herbs next to the mandrake root. They are powerful and can cause you to convulse and lose your senses. Do it now!"

The one thing Zaraquel was never used to was getting yelled at this way. Sure, her mom and dad would be angry at her for the stupid things she'd do, but this was different. It was more sinister to her. Not even Loquiel, her first love, would yell at her as the witch bitch does. She tossed the ingredients into the cauldron and watched them create a black smoke that rose above the pot. The mandrake root started crying near her, or at least that's what it sounded like it. Her hand reached for the root out of habit as if to soothe it, but the witch's hand came down quickly on hers.

"Not yet."

Zaraquel pulled her hand back and, in a whisper, said, "Bitch."

The witch either heard her or didn't. At this point, she didn't care anymore. If she received a punishment, so be it. Zaraquel wanted this teaching to be done so she could move forward with bringing Rae back. The bubbly brew began to smell, and she wrinkled her nose in disgust. The witch took a spoon to the brew and stirred it slowly.

"Angel, it's almost ready. Mandrake root is a powerful ingredient that witches use. I'm sure your teachers of light magic cautioned against some of its uses, but dark magic has strong capabilities. One such use is that the mandrake root mixed with specific herbs can call the devil himself to your side or be used in ecstasy, for starters. With these ingredients, you create a demon that will serve you. Hold the mandrake root carefully, don't break it. Gently lower it into the cauldron. Let it sink naturally, ignoring its cries."

Zaraquel held the mandrake as instructed and lowered it into the cauldron. The shrieks kept getting louder and louder, and she was tempted to throw it in, but she didn't. She had to get this spell right.

The witch handed her a stone. It was translucent, unlike the other stones she had seen in the garden or at the Order. Her hands felt the sides of the stone, and it felt strange to her touch, but there was a soft spot on it. She used her fingers to rub the spot to see why a hard stone had such a soft spot. Zaraquel noticed the witch watching her.

"That soft spot, Angel, is where the demon begins to take shape. The mandrake root will eventually fit inside the stone. You will see. This is another one of those dark magic spells that won't be taught to a light witch under normal circumstances. Take that spoon over there. Pour a small spoonful into the soft spot of the stone, one after another. Watch closely as it changes shape. While watching, you must repeat these words as you pour the first spoon onto the stone and the last. No words in between. These are the words. Listen closely."

"Wait! What will my demon look like? Will it live forever, or do I need to kill it? Tell me more about my future demon. Please, Anne."

"Your demon will live as long as you would like it to. You need to give your demon a name so you can control it. Like all demons, he will serve the master in the end. You are like his mother, in a way. The demon you create will do your bidding, but he will ultimately obey the master. We all do, whether we like it or not."

Zaraquel got cold, and a pain in her stomach made her scream, doubling over. The witch ran to her and tried to soothe her. Zaraquel started screaming in pain. It was agony.

What the hell is happening to me?

Then she noticed it. A vial was hidden behind the witch but was visible when she moved. The witch must've noticed her looking at the table, and her attitude changed. She became firm, demanding to know what Zaraquel was looking at.

"Nothing, Anne. It's just that I saw the empty vial over there, and I thought maybe…" Zaraquel needed to think of something quick. "I thought I made a mistake with the ingredients."

Anne looked at her with wonder, and Zaraquel stayed the course. The pain increased, and she finally collapsed again into the witch's arms. Though she was unconscious, her mind raced with hundreds of images. Zaraquel felt like she was an observer of these images, yet she wondered if this was what her mother's gift of sight was like.

The Tall Dark Man was hovering over a woman. She couldn't identify the woman, but she noticed something familiar. A marking. She only knew of one who had a marking like that. Rae. But how? She saw others in the background, witches, she assumed. Then she saw her dad chained at his feet. Zaraquel looked around at her vision, taking in everything she could. Demons, witches. Everywhere. She forced the vision to be gone. Instead, another one appeared. And another. It was never-ending. A while later, she assumed it all stopped.

*****

Sabre, Eastern Washington, Present Day

Sabre, Black Wind, and another elder sat around the fire discussing the curse. Several women stood to the side to tend to them. Malakai sat on one side of the fire, but the others and couldn't tell if he understood what they were doing or was getting accustomed to being a wolf. One of the women offered the wolf water and some food, and he played with the food but drank the water. By watching Malakai's behavior, Sabre knew he understood the sacrifice of not giving in to animal urges. He sat by Malakai and began to pet him.

"Brother, you need to eat. Strong Feather offered you food; it's not hunting. Eat, brother, for strength."

Turning to Black Wind, Sabre urged his plea to his brother."We need to think, brother! How do we defeat the dark witch? Brother Malakai can't remain in this state forever. In a past life, he was known as Giorgos, faithful and loyal to the queen. Just like he is today, he must be returned to her side."

Black Wind said, "I remember my great-great-grandfather telling me about the Hexham witches when I was a pup. The Tall Dark Man had his favorite witch of all of them. Elizabeth Hexham was her name. Her heart was pure darkness, a match for his. It is said that she bore many children, each within their own power. Raven's mother's line comes directly from Elizabeth's daughter, Alison. Her heart was not always black. She was as religious as they come until the Tall Dark Man seduced her. But I'm getting astray. Let me think a minute."

As Sabre listened, he was horrified at evil's presence in this world. As he thought about all the evil they had recently battled, he was pulled back when Black Wind began to speak again.

"The witch Elizabeth had a son. A fine son who would not follow the path of darkness. Instead, he was drawn to the light magic of the world. Elizabeth was full of hate, so she banished him from home, and he wandered the world. No one heard from him again until he met the Tall Dark Man himself. Let me see if I can remember the legend."

Black Wind grabbed a beer and took a large gulp before nodding to Sabre. Sabre couldn't wait, so he started asking, "Has anyone seen this male witch? I've never heard of a witch refusing to serve the Tall Dark Man."

Black Wind answered, "The son changed his name the moment he left the Hexham coven. He became known around the countryside as Phoenix because he rose from the ashes of his former life. If I remember the legend, he faced the Tall Dark Man and sought to free his family from evil. The two battled, and the Tall Dark Man cursed him. It is said that Phoenix was frozen and placed in a realm between life and death. The Tall Dark Man knew he couldn't kill a member of the Hexham line, so he placed him in the 'in-between,' as they call it. As far as anyone knows, Phoenix is the only one who can break any dark curse made by his family."

Sabre sat in disbelief as his heart sank at hearing the legend. He realized he had no choice but to embark on an adventure to find this realm. The one person he thought might know of this realm would be McPherson.

Pushing those thoughts out of his mind, Sabre said, "Black Wind, I need you and the others to watch Malakai. I am going to McPherson to seek his guidance on this legend, and to find the realm. I don't know when

I will return, but I must leave immediately. Malakai can't return to the queen in his current state."

Black Wind nodded as Sabre stood to begin his journey.

Chapter Seven
Secrets Revealed

Amber, Seattle Museum, Present Day

While Marcus was caring for and guarding Chloe, Amber rummaged around Malakai's office. She was thankful that Malakai never kept secrets from her and that their relationship gave her the courage to search through his office. Amber rummaged through his usual paperwork but noted how Malakai was such a neat freak. She ran her hands over the leather-bound notebook she gave him as a gift and smiled, remembering that day. Something urged her to look in the drawers. She opened the top drawers and discovered nothing out of the ordinary.

The last drawer caught her attention, however. Amber opened it and roamed her hands through the sides, the bottom, all over. She was unsure what she was looking for until her birthmark glowed, and as she ran her finger over it, she closed her eyes. She slowed her breathing until she could sense what her powers would show her.

Amber could see Malakai's last moves in this office which involved this drawer.

Malakai opened the end table in the far-right corner and removed a key. He then took a wrapped text, and as he opened the desk's bottom drawer, he used the key in a secret lock. He placed the book here, and as he closed it, he mouthed the words, "Show yourself to the queen."

The images faded. Amber repeated the steps she saw, and once the key was inserted, the secret panel opened and revealed the wrapped book that Malakai hid there. She removed the book from the cloth and stared at the cover. It had a symbol she didn't recognize, but a letter fell out as she opened the text.

Dearest Daughter,

We knew the day would come when you would rise to power, a power that the world would not understand. We did. We loved you so much and knew your destiny was far greater than that of anyone else we knew. Will you ever truly discover your heritage and full potential once we leave you? Know this, my darling daughter; seek the truth in your mother's line. Begin with her father, Talios, though you may be surprised by what you find. Search for the truth always but let your heart guide you. Till I see you again, sweet daughter. I did find this in our journeys to keep you safe. Perhaps these words will help you as we could not decipher them and give them to Malakai, your imprint.

Everything is connected. The Hexham warlock turned his back on his family and embraced the light. He met a teacher named Talios. This teacher guided his student, and he was born again till he met his family's sire—the Tall Dark Man. Phoenix is the key to understanding your potential. Talios has a secret cave where Phoenix would leave his precious findings from around the world. You will find the cave in a dark forest, but your heart must be pure to invoke the light.

With all my love,
Your father, Nikoli

Amber finished reading the letter, and blood tears ran down her cheeks. It was the first item she had ever touched that her father had left for her. She took the letter and the book, locked the office, and went to find the others.

***

The Tall Dark Man, 1600s, England

He stood in the shadows, watching Alison Hexham teach her daughter the craft. She was learning the same spells he had taught his Elizabeth the years before. Alison created demons from the tiniest pebbles; soon, her young daughter did the same. The Tall Dark Man smiled at how well this line of witches bore the fruition of his darkest desires. He decided it was time to appear, as it had been many years since he saw Alison last.

Alison noticed him immediately and bowed in reverence to him. He smiled as she said, "Master. It's been so long since you've graced me with your presence. May I present to you my daughter from the last time you visited? She has grown in power. This is my daughter, Charlotte."

He nodded in approval and said, "It looks like she has received the power from you and your mother. She will do me a great honor when she is older. What can she create at her age?"

Alison looked at her daughter and said, "Show the master your power."

The child wove her hands together, and in a soft voice, she commanded the pebbles to change shape and transform into a small army of demons. Even though the demons were the size of pebbles, he could see that this child was powerful. The demons were from a child's mind, so it was no concern that the little demons were dancing and playing on the ground. However, with a snap of her fingers, the demons circled him and knelt. Obviously, the child was remarkable in her power that the demons obeyed the child. The Tall Dark Man smiled and reached down to pick up one of the demons. The little demon, the size of a pebble, held onto his thumb so tight that he could feel its strength. With the tip of his index finger, he rubbed the little demon to see if it would crumble; it did not. The demon started giggling, and that's when he saw the innocence of a child in this magic. He wondered at the thought of her power growing while she was so young. As he studied the demon, the child tugged on his black coat and said, "I know you."

"Do you, child? How do you know me?"

The little girl looked up at him, and her eyes narrowed. She spoke again, this time in a voice he hadn't heard before.

"Two children born, one for the light and the other for the dark. The child of the light will always guide the queen, while the child of the dark will seek to destroy her. You are the child of the dark. The queen will rise one day to destroy you, but that will pass through her scepter. Her life for the scepter is the cost to end your days."

The Tall Dark Man got the most peculiar feeling that he knew the voice that spoke, but he shook it off because it was impossible. Then the little girl spoke again.

"You hear my voice. You recognize the words. Don't you, Sammael? I can hear your thoughts. What you seek has not yet been born. Your key to fulfilling your destiny comes from this child's line, not those before her. The child's mate bears the mark of the serpent. Through their union will come a family of witches to strengthen the power of the Hexham coven into something more. Through the years, a daughter with hair as black as a raven, a birthmark on her cheek, and an undeniable power will be your weapon against the light. Guide this child to find the one who bears the mark, or your prophecy will fail."

He listened and waited for more but saw a confused child before him. He heard what was spoken and knew he must do as commanded. Turning to Alison, he smiled.

"These demons are just the smallest indication of the child's ability. The child has remarkable strengths in her power. Other than you, has there been anyone else to teach this child?"

Alison shook her head. "Just me, master. She is young but she has the sight. She can see things. She speaks of things yet to come, but as you saw, she creates things by simply weaving her hands together, but much of her weaving has not been taught to her yet. She simply knows."

"And these demons she creates. Can they be larger?"

Alison shrugged. "I do not know, master. When she creates, things are usually child-sized, to match her visions."

"You have honored me with your daughter's power. Now honor me in other ways."

Alison knew her duty well and led him into the house. The Tall Dark Man took his time with his witch. Of all the Hexham witches he bedded, Alison was the most sensual for him. He undressed and ran his fingers down her arms, watching as she removed his clothes. When she kissed him, he felt completely different. It was as if he had lost his thoughts of the prophecy, and his mind focused on her body. Her curves, soft skin, and pouty lips reminded him of Elizabeth, his favorite witch, but Alison was his one witch with the power of seduction.

She removed her dress and let it fall to her feet. He watched her intently as she ran her fingers through her hair and bit one of her fingers as if to lure him. Alison raised her hands to try to remove his hat, but with one hand, he stopped her.

"Master, show me your face. Let your witch free you of the burdens on your shoulder. Let me pleasure you, free you for a moment in time."

As she kissed him passionately, he lost his way in that kiss. She removed his hat and ran her fingers against his face. With her hands, she touched his body, and he succumbed to her embrace. He was no longer in control. Alison began to nibble at his neck, and he moaned. He knew her power over men. Her power over him.

"Bed me, witch. Command me, witch. Only here will I give you control over me."

Once he said those words, he was lost to her sensuality and desires. Alison took her cue, pushed him down on the bed, and straddled him like always. Her mouth lingered on his torso until he moaned with desire. Then with a flick of her tongue, she began to lick him, making him squeal with fervor. Alison knew her skills and prolonged the intensity until it drove him mad. He couldn't take it much longer with her oral fixation, so he took control of her body. It was as much a game for him as it was for her.

The Tall Dark Man sought his pleasure until he spilled his seed inside her, and not only did he make her moan, but he bound her to him once more.

***

Mary, Seattle, Present Day

Mary was settling in the new home the master had rented for her and the witch for their assignment. The baby was already napping in his room connected to the witch's room in a Jack and Jill style. The witch, Tabitha, had shown her the master bedroom, which made her giddy with excitement. It was beautiful, but on the bed was a note from him, reminding her of her assignment and that while she was above ground, he would not interfere as long as she was successful. The last sentence stood out the most: *You may take your time befriending Chloe but don't take **too** long.*

After reading that sentence, she knew he meant to get started immediately and not spend all her time with Elijah. She approached Tabitha and said, "Could I take my baby for a walk? I need to get familiar with things here, which is strange to me now. It's unlike what I remember; the master never let me go above ground."

"You can walk, but the baby must remain in my care. You can be a mother to him in this house only but not on the outside. My instructions are clear, and you must complete the mission."

Mary was beginning to get angry. "You're telling me I'm still a prisoner despite serving the master in this mission? Give me my baby, you… you… witch bitch from Hell."

Tabitha ignored her protests, and Mary could no longer control her rage. She began to clench her fingers, and without thinking, a ball of fire emerged from them. Mary aimed it at Tabitha and felt her temperature rising as her anger consumed her.

The fire missed Tabitha, but she reached for the baby and yelled for Mary to control her anger, but she refused to listen. She started to weave her hands together and tried to create another ball of flames to throw at Tabitha. The sound of Elijah crying wasn't enough to subdue Mary.

"Stop, Mary, or I will call the master. He will end you for this."

"I will do the master's bidding but not take your orders."

Mary secretly hoped that her watching the coven of witches over the centuries would prove enough for what she was about to do. As she weaved the magic in her hands, she decided to whisper a spell she heard Raven once say when punishing another witch for willful contempt. That witch lost her magic – it was more than a binding spell. She whispered the words and directed her hands toward Tabitha. The magic encircled the witch and tightened its grip on her. Tabitha screamed, "What did you do to me?"

"I transferred your magic and your knowledge of spells to me, and I will return them once I am done with the master's bidding. I do not need a babysitter."

Tabitha just stared at her. "How did you become powerful? You didn't have the training in advanced witchcraft."

Mary smiled. "Years of sitting and watching, playing the stupid girl he captured centuries ago—years of deceiving you and your coven of witches. I will take revenge for my husband's death by doing the master's will, and my son is mine. Not yours."

Grabbing Elijah, Mary glanced at a crying shell of a former powerful witch. Before leaving the room, she took one more look at Tabitha and told her to clean up the place. From the corner of her eye, she saw Tabitha crawl along the floor before rising to do as she was bid. The satisfaction of power over the witch gave Mary the confidence she had lacked previously when suffering at their hands.

Mary could hear Tabitha cursing about her new predicament.

"Mary, you will burn for this. I'll see to it."

***

Raven, Seattle, Present Day

Raven and Arioch searched the estate grounds, trying hard not to be discovered. What she saw amazed her. Groups of all races working together, practicing their fighting moves, and breathing the same air with no definitive hierarchical system. She motioned for Arioch to follow her, and they found a way into the mansion undetected.

"Seek what you need to track the wolf, demon. Find me once you catch his scent. I have to find the witch's room."

They went their separate ways, but Raven decided to be fast about it. The last thing she needed was someone powerful in this mansion to break her hold on Arioch again. Once she found the witch's room, she looked at the vials, spell books, and other exciting items. There was a particular book she was looking for: the Tudor coven's Book of Shadows. Raven didn't plan on taking it, but she wanted to see the spells of light that could be used against Chloe. If it would help the master with his vengeance, she was willing to do anything.

As she crept from room to room, she was careful not to make a sound. Then she saw two servants round the corner. She ran into the nearest room; luckily, it was Chloe's room. Rummaging through the myriad of items, Raven spotted an older-looking chest in the corner, covered with a multicolored blanket. Once she unlocked the chest with magic, she saw her coven's artifacts—parchments of spells, incantations, and a family tree. She saw Chloe's name and followed the lines up to the head matriarch. Then she saw the name. Sarah Good. That's why the master wanted her power badly. Chloe's line began with Sarah Good. Next to Elizabeth Hexham, born centuries before, Sarah Good's power was unmatchable by any other light witch. As Raven looked closer, she saw the names of her vampire husband and the angel. Carefully folding the parchment, she placed it in her pocket to give to the master. He would be most pleased.

Still rummaging through the trunk, she finally found the Book of Shadows for Chloe's coven. Raven knew she wouldn't be able to touch the book, so she used the power of Elizabeth Hexham that flowed through her to open the book. At first, the book didn't give, so Raven amplified her power.

"Liber coventatis, paginas tuas quaere alica lucis contra tenebras."

The book began to shake, and with immense power, the pages turned to the most powerful light spell the coven knew—the power of light against darkness. Raven read the spell and memorized it. Then with another spell, she changed the words so that if Chloe used the spell, it would backfire on her and weaken her, making her easier to control and bring to the master.

She left to search for Arioch, and once she found him, she read his mind. She spoke to him, and they left the mansion to search for the wolf. Raven was determined to bring the wolf to the master in his animal form, where he could be used against the queen. She was not about to fail the task the master gave her. The penalty of disobedience or failure could cost her life.

142

Chapter Eight
Darkness Approaches

Kawika (David) Kekahuna, Honolulu, Present Day

Kawika was walking along Kalakaua Avenue, getting his steps in after work. It was a beautiful evening as he headed toward Kapi´olani Park. He usually sat at home reading his books on Hawaiian history, making him one of the state's leading experts on Hawaiian culture. Something inside him was pointing him in this direction. He knew his family history well and the power wielded by his ancestors. It would be no use answering this call.

Once he entered the public park, he saw many tourists enjoying the land's beauty. That was one of the many reasons he loved his career. He was sharing his culture and island with people who could appreciate it. As he walked closer to the beach, something caught his attention. A vision inside his mind appeared as he tried to move closer to see what it was. Kawika saw the kaimoni approaching a group of people. The area was dark and secluded, but he could make out Diamond Head in the background. His vision changed to a beautiful young woman with red hair surrounded by giant wolves. The fire burned around her, and he saw the kaimoni approaching her. Her eyes were green, but they seemed to narrow as she raised her hand towards the kaimoni. Kawika didn't see what happened next because someone bumped into him. As he regained his focus, he realized that the man was possessed. Using his unique gifts, Kawika tried to see in the man's soul and saw the kaimoni that possessed him. Kawika began to breathe heavily, the same as he did during one of his panic attacks.

His phone vibrated in his pocket, and he looked at the number: his kupuna kāne. Kawika wondered if he sensed something was amiss.

"Grandfather. I mean, kupuna kāne. I…"

"No time for small talk. Come home. I need the entire o'hana at the house. We must prepare."

Before Kawika could say anything more, his grandfather hung up. Kawika's family were descendants of the kahunas, the Hawaiian priests, and they held a sacred oath to the land and its people – the native Hawaiians. The possessed man had already disappeared, and there was no use searching for him. He had to go to the family home. As he headed toward the family home, the image of the young red-headed woman never left his mind. He was determined to seek her out, but there wasn't much to go on. Kawika would research until he sought the answers he wanted.

***

Zaraquel, The Witch's Cottage, Present Day

The next day, Zaraquel was determined to create her demon with or without the witch's teachings. So far, demon after demon has died upon creation, and she couldn't understand why. The witch didn't notice her today, which meant that Zaraquel was left alone. Then she saw why. Her wings were darker than the other day.

"Damnit!" Zaraquel became upset at the thought of losing her balance. Remembering the words from Nimue, she breathed in and slowly exhaled. Her temper was beginning to even out once more. Determined to create a demon, she thought about the spell and began changing it around. The ingredients remained the same, not the

words or the order she put them. She was determined to create a demon to serve only her.

Once the mandrake was placed in the cauldron, Zaraquel breathed slowly. Closing her eyes, she pictured her mother, the strongest light witch she knew. Then the image of her father, the vampire, came to the surface, and she could feel a power within her from that image. Her wings began to tingle, and she giggled with delight. At first, she was afraid she would capture the witch's attention, but Anne didn't appear. Zaraquel began to sense something.

Looking for the witch throughout the cottage, she eventually found her deep in conversation, but no one was there. The room was one the witch always told Nimue and Zaraquel never to enter. Both always wondered why, in fact, Nimue sometimes teased that the forbidden room was where Anne secretly became a donkey because she could be such an ass. Zaraquel would always laugh at that. Careful not to be seen, Zaraquel whispered the spell of invisibility that Uncle Mac had taught her and Rae before. She peered around the corner once more and listened. She wanted to see what was really happening and she couldn't from her spot. Zaraquel began to move into the room. The witch kept talking. She gasped at what she was hearing.

"When you have subdued the angel in a trance, send me a message. Mother of the devil fits with all the power I have given you. Subdue the angel and her power till I arrive to claim her. Knowing that her vampire father will surrender to me has me intrigued as to why. Remember whom you serve, witch."

"Master, the angel, is learning the dark magic for you to control her, and she must master the essential spells that will bend her will to you. They are complex spells, but she will learn and use them. She will be yours, and I am nothing more than your humble servant."

"I am pleased. I will send you another witch from the coven to aid you. I am not a patient man."

"Thank you, master."

They continued talking, but Zaraquel had heard all she needed to hear, and it dawned on her. Learning the dark magic was costing her more than her wings. She hoped her mother's strength and tenacity flowed in her blood. Zaraquel returned to the cauldron and removed the spell of invisibility. She gathered her strength and power to create one more demon before giving up. Changing the words around for the spell and calling upon the power of her mother's ancestors, the stone began to rise from the cauldron and take shape. The mandrake root was forming inside it. The stone began to change shape and color.

Slowly, the demon was forming before her eyes. The stone turned a bright orange, almost like the color of fire. It was minutes before the spell finished creating the demon as it stood before her. The demon was a young woman, who looked about her age. She had fire red hair, probably because of the bright orange stone color. Her eyes were also red. She definitely would stand out if seen in the human world. Zaraquel started to giggle just a little bit. She looked like a young woman, but her skin was different. Her skin appeared to look like snakeskin but when Zaraquel touched her arm, it was smooth. The demon looked beautiful, though, to Zaraquel. She was impressed with her spell. Her magic worked but at what cost? That had yet to be seen.

Zaraquel rubbed her eyes and remembered what Anne had said. She must name her demon, and she had to find a way that the demon would not obey the Tall Dark Man.

The demon moved its head from side to side, staring straight at Zaraquel. It made her uncomfortable, but she raised her hand to point straight ahead, and the demon mimicked her move. Zaraquel produced a rose from a spell and offered it to the demon. The demon didn't take it at first. Then she opened her hand, hoping the demon would mimic it, and it did. The demon took the rose.

"Demon," she said, "I am your master. You will listen and obey only me. I command you by naming you Garnet Rose. Hear your name and obey me."

The demon's eyes flickered and nodded. The demon even spoke!

"I, Rose."

"Garnet Rose. I am Zara. Your mother, in a way."

The demon tilted its head as if it understood. Zaraquel smiled at her creation and said, "You're a female demon. I want you to be strong, powerful, cunning, and loyal to me. Understand?" With a flick, she cast the words onto the demon.

Garnet Rose smiled.

"I understand, mother."

Zaraquel decided she would master the dark side of magic, but she would not remain here if what Anne says is true. She had to save her father somehow and bring Rae back. But how will she do both? Garnet Rose tilted her head in the same way that Zaraquel was doing while deep in thought.

"I will help you, mother. To save father and bring Rae back."

Zaraquel looked at her demon with narrowing eyes. "How can you know that's what I want? Can you read my mind, Garnet Rose?"

"I am linked to you, mother, and only you. I can sense you, read your mind and protect you. You wanted me to be those things. And I'm beautiful too. Just like you wanted."

Zaraquel took a deep breath. "Oh boy. This better work."

***

Marcus, Seattle Museum, Present Day

Marcus paced the office while Chloe was sleeping. He made a deal with the devil and was unsure of how to free himself of it. As he thought of why he did it, peace fell over him because he knew both Zaraquel and Chloe would be safe. All this to bring back Rae. The more he thought about it, the more he realized he needed McPherson to guide him. Without Michael, he was lost in the prophecy. As he left Chloe asleep, he decided to help Amber.

He located the queen outside Malakai's office and motioned for her to return inside. As he entered the large room, he started to sniff the air. He loved Malakai like a brother, but damn, he hated the smell of dogs. Marcus wondered how Amber could stand the smell when she was with Malakai.

Amber crinkled her nose and asked, "You smell it too? It smells like Malakai but with something else. It's not his scent, and I never smelled anything so foul like that before."

"Yeah, Amber, it's pungent. Coming from the bookshelf."

Marcus and Amber stood before the bookshelf, and Marcus smelled the air again. He could smell the strong odor from a particular book and the smell of dogs and something else. Grabbing it from the shelf, he opened it. He thumbed through the pages until one caught his eye. He knew it didn't belong in the museum due to the wolf symbol.

The words "History of Delaware Clan" stood out. He read the page before reading aloud to Amber. Marcus knew that Malakai was from Delaware and that was Amber's birthplace. To find the queen, he had to do homework on her at Michael's request.

He quietly read the words on the page, "*Evil will destroy the Delaware clan as prophesied. A daughter will be born to this clan with many lives lived.*" Marcus continued reading. He remembered Malakai telling them about how his clan was destroyed after Nikoli and Miriam left. He returned to a wasteland. But Malakai said that the stench in the air was evil and ancient. Marcus breathed deeply. He skimmed the rest and started flipping through the pages before returning to the page he began with.

Marcus read the paragraph silently once more before letting Amber hear what was in the book. Once she heard the words, she cried, but then she pulled out the letter that her father had written. She handed the letter to Marcus as she turned away to sit down. Marcus read the letter, and Chloe barged into their room as he finished. He saw that she was still weak but standing.

Chloe yelled "Don't touch that book! It's tainted with evil. I can sense the evil from here."

Marcus instantly dropped that book, but not before his skin started burning. He felt like he was walking in daylight but wasn't. Marcus began to wonder if he was able to touch the book for a bit before burning because he made a deal with the Tall Dark Man. He practically gave himself to evil to save his family. To save them all. The blisters began to form. He was in agony and was usually able to withstand pain, even when caught in the daylight, but this was unbearable. He screamed and fell to his knees.

Chloe saw her Marcus fall and said, "Amber, did you touch the book too?"

"No, Chloe. I was about to, but I didn't. I don't know why I didn't. I wanted to."

Marcus was still screaming.

From the book, a shadow emerged. Marcus realized that it was dark magic. The Tall Dark Man's voice emanated from the shadow.

"I see you got my message, vampire. It won't be long before you realize your fate, your wife's fate, and the queen's. I will have my vengeance. All I needed was a little appetizer to lure you all in. Your skin will be made whole in time. It is a reminder of your agreement with me, vampire. You can choose the time of your fate but not the fate of your daughter and wife. The queen will fall when all her warriors are stripped from her. Time is the only adversary I have because you will fall to me one way or another. You have all started to fall and didn't even realize it."

Marcus turned to face Chloe and noticed her face had changed. She was angry, probably at what they had all just heard. He tried to calm her down but could barely move because his skin was in intense pain.

Barely controlling her fury, Chloe said, "Your agreement with the Tall Dark Man? OUR daughter, Marcus? What the fuck did you do?"

He hung his head in shame and looked at the queen and then at his wife. As he struggled with the pain, he said, "I did what I had to… for Zara to learn dark magic and to keep you safe. I… learned that she needs light and dark magic… to ascend higher and not just to bring Rae back. She doesn't fully understand her role, but I thought she was destined… for much more as I studied some of the books with McPherson after the battle. Her soul is the key to destroying him. The prophecy… is what I studied for centuries with Michael. It was our secret. It's in the book. Michael was sworn to protect the book. I knew of it and where it was kept in the library. I kept this secret, thinking it was over… but I was wrong. The prophecy is unfinished. If it ends as written… darkness will prevail over the earth. All of us supernatural creatures will be under his control if an angel… with both light and dark… does not rise to accept her destiny. The prophecy was not about Amber. Amber was the key to unlocking the greatest supernatural of all. There's more, but I can't tell you here. Either the pain is subsiding, or I'm managing it. We need to get back to the estate. Then I will tell you everything. I need Jerome's help. I read the book. I know its language from Kabos, as did Michael."

What he said must've caught Amber's attention since she said, "The book I found in the library! That must be the same book you are talking about. I could only read bits of it, not much. We need to get there, Chloe. Fast. Give us a lift in that special way you have, witch best friend?" Marcus noticed her wink at Chloe.

Chloe must've understood his wink because she simply said, "Let's fly!" and the next thing Marcus knew, they were all back at the estate. And with the books.

Chapter Nine
The Dead Comes Calling

Night Marchers, Ancient Hawaii

On the nights of Kanaloa, the deadliest warriors roam the islands once more. This particular night, Keino decided to leave her hut for fresh air. She was nervous about marrying the fisherman Kalauwihi, but her father was adamant about the union. The union was to honor the god Kanaloa, ruler of the oceans, and bless him as a kahuna. She was the first daughter of a powerful kahuna. As she walked away from her hut, she saw the warriors and heard their chants.

Instead of returning home to her parents, she crouched in the foliage where she couldn't be seen. She wanted to see the night marchers, the huaka'i pō. Keino held her breath as they walked past her, but a little animal ran past her and stopped in front of a night marcher who stepped on the animal, causing it to squeal. Keino let out a small scream, and it was loud enough to get the attention of the night marchers. One of them came right towards her.

Keino screamed in the loudest voice she could. The night marcher covered her with his body. Her finger tried to touch him to see if he was still a man, but her finger poked the air. She knew that she would die violently because she looked at them. Quickly she knelt on the ground, trying to put her face down in respect, but it was too late.

One of the night marchers saw her and spoke. "You will live, wahine, but I will curse you till you die. I will haunt you while you live. You will be marked as an evil spirit if you are known to man. Surrender your life to us; we will leave you in peace until death calls for you."

Keino wanted to live, but that meant marrying Kalauwihi without knowing him as a wife. She nodded, and from that moment, her soul became dark. Her light was no more. Keino did not want to tell her father, but she had no choice. The shame she would have brought on herself might also have caused her death.

Her father, Kalua, listened to her. Then he honored the god Kanaloa by telling her she would honor the night marchers' command. The wedding was called off, and Keino became the night marchers' dark kahuna from that day forward.

***

Malia, Honolulu, Present Day

Malia was worried about her boss and friend, Kawika. She called him Mr. Kekahuna when they were in the office, but over the last six months, the two of them found that Malia's oʻhana were royal descendants of King Kamehameha while working on some research. This carefully guarded secret protected her from some native Hawaiians raised against the old idea of unifying the islands. Even though this was an honor, her tūtū always cautioned her so that she could fit in and live life to its fullest. She knew that Kawika had kept this secret since the day they discovered it. During this time, she remembered how Kawika told her that she wasn't the only one with family secrets but he left it at that.

She tried to reach him on his cell phone, but he never picked up. Before she could dial again, her tūtū called.

"Hello, tūtū," Malia said. "Are you ok? I'm headed to Mom and Dad's, but if you need anything, let me know."

"Malia, I need you to come here now. We need to awaken your ancestral spirit, and I sense something evil is coming, and you are of the bloodline."

"I don't understand. Look, I'm going home. I had a

long day at work. Can it wait?"

"NO! Granddaughter, you must come now. Come and join us; your o´hana waits. Even your father."

Malia hung up and turned her jeep around. She couldn't disappoint her father by not listening to her tūtū. She was raised on honor. Plus, it made her wonder because Kawika said the same thing – evil was coming! She drove about two hours before reaching the other side of the island, courtesy of the unusual traffic. As she continued down the Pali, she began to see why. Cars lined up alongside the road, and the drivers stood outside staring into the valley. Malia couldn't resist her curiosity and joined the other drivers in their observations. She strained her eyes to see the dark specks at the bottom of the valley. When she couldn't determine what they were, she returned to the jeep and found her binoculars. She kept all sorts of tools in her jeep due to her internship. Kawika told her to be prepared because she may find a relic even while walking on the beach!

Malia focused her binoculars even more, and then she saw them! Ghost warriors from the dead! Then she noticed the people had no idea what they were looking at. All they could see was a bunch of pigs running around the cliff, which also was something that usually did not happen at the Pali. She tried to recall her

Hawaiian history and folklore. She closed her eyes and silently prayed to Kāne to keep the people safe. *It is always about the land and the people. Protect the land and the people.* She felt something warm touch her shoulder, but when she turned around, nothing was there.

Think, damnit, think! Malia's head was spinning, and she heard an inner voice call.

"Daughter. Daughter. I am with you. Why do you not pray to me, the fire and volcano goddess?"

Malia thought she must be exhausted because why would a voice call her daughter and represent themselves as the goddess Pele? She decided to answer and see what would happen.

"I listen to you, goddess Pele. You are goddess Pele, are you not? These ghost warriors have entered your valley. I can see them, but no one else can. Why?"

"You are the daughter of Pele. One of them. Born of ancient times but placed in a long slumber until one of the gods woke you to return you to me. Dark times come, and I must protect the people and the land. Beware the man that comes. He is the bringer of death."

Malia felt the warmth on her shoulder once more. This time, as she turned around, she saw a young version of Pele. More beautiful than all the paintings and pictures depicted the goddess. She smiled at Pele. Malia always knew the legend of Pele that she would appear either as a young maiden or an old woman. She forgot the people around her and knelt in respect to Pele.

"Rise, daughter. I accept your respect to me. I ask you to help me protect the land and its people. Don't forget the pigs too. I bless you child, more than you know."

Malia did not understand what she heard but watched the ghost warriors, the kaimoni, walk the Pali valley. It was a matter of time before they came to higher ground.

She looked at the crowds and waved them down, saying, "The pigs are just loose in search of food and water. It's that time of year. Folks, let's get back on the road. Nothing more to see here but just a hungry pack of pigs!"

People reluctantly returned to their vehicles and continued to cross the Pali. Malia gave another look at the valley and saw the ghost warriors continue to walk the land. She began worrying and decided her family better answer some questions she was starting to have about everything. Before returning to her jeep, she glanced again and realized the ghost warriors were coming closer. The feeling of Pele still stayed with her and she smiled. She felt honored that the goddess would appear to her.

***

Malia finally reached her tūtū's home and saw many cars lined up in the driveway and the street. She always loved visiting, but today was not one of those days. Too many weird things were happening that she couldn't explain.

Taking a deep breath, Malia opened the door. People she didn't know were walking around the house, and as she searched for her father, she bumped into a few strangers. They seemed to have a panicked look, enough to tell her that something was going on. Her tūtū found her and clasped her hands, saying, "Malia, we must talk, but not here. Come, join your father and me in the other room."

She thought, *Can this day get any stranger*? But as obedient as she was, she had questions after seeing what she saw. Malia lived with the secrets kept from her, but now that she was an intern and soon-to-be graduate of the University of Hawaii, it was time to know the truth.

Tūtū began speaking, even as Malia hugged her father—something she always did, no matter how old she was.

He said, "The dead are walking the land. Evil is in the air. What did Mr. Kekahuna tell you?"

Perplexed by the question, she still answered. "Nothing, tūtū. We worked, and there was this relic that we were trying to catalog. It is made of koa wood and seems like a lost relic from the god Kū. I couldn't tell much more from the relic because Mr. Kekahuna got ill once he touched it. What are you not telling me? I've already had enough crazy things happen today, even at the Pali on the way here. I'm not in the mood for games, Dad."

Malia could tell that she upset them both, but enough was enough. She wanted to study the history and folklore of Hawaii, which she went to the university for, but she wanted to see the world outside of the islands.

Malia's father, Lono, coughed and sat down. Her grandmother joined him.

Tūtū said, "It's time to tell her, son. She must know before the demons come."

"Malia, sit. Listen to what I tell you, but I know you will have many questions. Just hear what I have to say first."

"Okay."

It sounded like the same speech they tried to tell her when she was about fourteen. Regardless, she was not their biological daughter but was loved and part of the o´hana. Malia sat down, just like she had done years ago, to learn more about her truth. The hidden truth.

Lono said, "Your mother and I found you when we

were coming home. You were walking along the Pali, so you probably loved always going there to think when things got tough. You were about three years old. We took you to H.P.D. No one knew of a missing child. The detectives were all nice. Then again, the Honolulu Police are family. Social Services let us foster you until we adopted you—that much. But you don't know that when we brought you here for the first time, tūtū and her friends could sense something about you. When we brought you to the Pali for the first time since we found you, tūtū came with us. She called to the valley for help, and an old woman appeared before her. It was madame Pele…"

Malia couldn't believe what she was hearing. *Madame Pele? People had a feeling about me?* It was too much for her to handle, so she did what she did best. Ran out of the house and into her jeep. She drove off into the evening.

***

The Tall Dark Man, Underground, Present Day

He sat once again in his throne room. It had been several days since Tabitha checked in to give him a report. Mary was always obedient; now that she had the

165

child, Valentine's son, in her arms, she would only be more compliant. Thoughts began to consume him, and he decided his impatience was doing him no good. He read more about the ancient texts regarding the angel becoming his bride. The thought of her power becoming his was satisfying.

Alone in the room with his texts and parchments, he sat at the table and grabbed the parchment about the angel. He deciphered it further than before.

> *When the angel's wings lie black as night, her soul is no longer of the light. She will embrace the dark lord in all his glory and give birth to a beast that will unleash fire and hell onto the world. The world will perish, the queen will fall, and there will be no reconciliation as once prophesied.*

His smile made him hungrier for his plans to work, but patience and timing were critical. First, he needed the stone demons to be created. He needed his army to be larger, stronger, and deadlier than the queen's. The Tall Dark Man needed the book that Machiel took centuries ago. And the Stone of the Damned. As he continued reading, he realized that this vengeance was beginning. Everything was falling into place like pieces on a chessboard. He just had to wait until he could look into the queen's eyes and say the sweet words, "Checkmate," as she died.

Patience was never his fortitude, so he revisited Tituba. He had no love for her, but she was beautiful and good at bearing demons. He wanted to implant his seed once more.

He entered the room and saw that she was still restrained to the bed. Previously, he sent witches to care for her and to make her ready once more for him. She wiggled against the restraints, begging to be free and touch him. He smiled at her and removed his clothing once more as he said, "You will be free to touch me, little witch. But you will earn that privilege. This time there can be no failure on your body to carry my seed. Do you understand?"

Tituba looked at him with a solemn look and nodded. He was never cruel to her before, but something inside him told her that a traitor among his witches had turned her against him. The Tall Dark Man touched her cheek and let his hand run down her shoulders, gliding over her abdomen. He drew an invisible, upside-down pentagram with a finger and pricked her skin using a fingernail. Blood began to trickle down, and he whispered a spell to ensure his seed would not die. Hovering over her, he spread her legs apart with his frame and placed his member in her again. She screamed in pleasure as he spilled his seed. Remaining inside for a few additional minutes to be sure his spell would hold, he looked into her eyes. He received no pleasure from her anymore like he used to. His bodily needs would be serviced by all the other obedient witches as he had no further use for her if she birthed his hunter.

"Master. I am obedient to your will. Use me as you see fit."

"Well done, Tituba. You are learning your place once more. I will send the witches in to clean you and dress you finely. You will be free as long as my seed grows inside you."

Back in his throne room, he watched several of the witches and wondered if Raven had the power to bring back someone familiar to the queen but deadly enough to serve him without fail this time. He knew Raven was on her mission with Arioch, but damn, he wanted to know if she could bring him back. He would have to wait but decided to visit the witch's cottage to see the angel himself. The Tall Dark Man found himself lusting after her, which was unusual for him.

***

Kawika Kekahuna, Honolulu, Present Day

Kawika sat before his grandfather and listened as he told the tale of the kaimoni returning when evil was active in the world. Kawika was a descendant of one of the greatest kahunas in the islands, long before the time of Kamehameha. Kawika was dumbfounded as he listened to his kupuna kāne. His mind was spinning, and he wondered if this was how Malia, his intern, felt when he was talking about the kaimoni.

"Kawika, it's in your blood. Your blood is sacred to the gods of Hawaii. Listen to your instinct. You can call the gods through ancient prayers if you need them. Legends speak of a queen. I don't remember my father or grandfather telling me when she would be born, but in all the world, there would be a queen to bring unification to all. There were stories of a queen based in Seattle who could be the one, like Kamehameha, to unite all. You will need her because the god Kū will not allow peace. Evil is coming. There is someone that the spirits of the land are calling for. She is not a native Hawaiian, but she is powerful. She defeated this evil once before with her oʻhana. A powerful family. A supernatural family."

"What do you mean?"

"Boy, you no listen to me. Get your slippah and kill da B-52 bombah. Then I talk more."

His grandfather was coughing, and one thing Kawika learned is that his grandfather loved to speak in pidgin, the popular language of the islands. Obedient, he took his shoe and killed the flying cockroach before his grandfather could get upset more than he was. He was intrigued by who this woman sorcerer could be, but his grandfather began smoking before he could ask anything else. After a few minutes, his grandfather spoke again.

"I can read your mind, Kawika. You forget who I am. She is the queen of all supernatural creatures like us, and we are kahunas. Bring her to the islands to defeat this evil. You will know her from her past lives. Do your homework, boy. Find Illyris, and the rest will fall into place. Pray to the god Kāne, Pele, and others that they give you strength for the upcoming."

Kawika knew his grandfather tired quickly, so he finished paying his respects to him, tidied up his home, and left so he could work on finding this queen.

Chapter Ten
Past Sins

Illyris, Ancient Greece

Illyris grew tired of the constant battle between her and the king's lapdog, Gerard. Between Gerard and that wretched man Mailik. A day didn't go by in which she wasn't confronted with her path of reconciliation between her race and the wolves. Illyris, once known as Bircenna, embraced the memories of her former life and used the courage she had received from Domator's love as the strength to endure what came next.

She would seek out the druids and other magic creatures. Illyris knew she would need their aid to save the wolves. She once loved the king, but when he set fire to her for her friendship with them, she knew that her strength lay in all who would stand with her. Then the

Covenant also sought to destroy her spirit, her choice for the wolves, especially for Giorgos. It was nothing but silence on news of the Covenant.

It had been months since Mailik had informed her of the Covenant and their dark intentions to continue to force the wolves into slavery. Giorgos and Illyris were determined to save the wolves from fate when she sensed something she couldn't explain. Instead of calling Giorgos for his help, she followed the shadow that intrigued her.

Illyris ran through the streets of Greece while chasing the shadow. She reached out to the others, and before anyone could help her, Malik confronted her and said, "You know the king had been patient and tolerant of your friendship with those dogs, but those still loyal to him will stop you. You can't save them all without sacrificing yourself in the process. However, I will make you this agreement. Surrender to me, and your loyal dog can live out his days, and I will only drain you of your blood little by little so that you will live. You will live but not the life you thought you would. The Covenant does not support you."

Illyris laughed and said, "The king trusted you. And you seek to destroy me just like him. Not today, in this lifetime, and not in the next either. Why don't you surrender to me instead?" Illyris snarled and decided it was time for a kill.

He chuckled at her and said, "The master will eventually kill you all. His prophecy will come true; your blood will let him rise above all. This has nothing to do with the king, and the Covenant already serves the master."

Illyris looked puzzled, and Mailik laughed more.

"Foolish woman. You didn't know that eventually, everyone will turn against you."

Illyris jumped on his shoulders and sank her teeth into his flesh. She twisted her hands around his head until it detached from his body with a crack. She wasn't satisfied with the news about the Covenant not leaving her alone, but that did not deter her from saving the wolves.

***

Raven Hexham, Seattle, Present Day

As Raven followed Arioch, her mind reflected on the past. Stories of her matriarch generations before her were something she always enjoyed hearing as a child. Charlotte was Alison's daughter, and Raven's line of powerful witches was born through her union with the

173

man who bore the serpent's mark. The man in all their stories was never heard from again, and Raven often wondered who he was.

Having caught up with Arioch, she convinced him to get in the car she had access to and drive to find the wolf. It would be much faster than on foot, especially since she couldn't sense him in Seattle. Before they left the parking lot, Raven used her powers. Arioch was like a child and seemed fascinated with everything he saw.

Raven wove her hands and conjured a bird. A raven. Just like her name. She sent the black raven to fly east and find the wolf. Raven even allowed him to send her images of where the wolf could be found. She watched the raven fly until she could no longer see it anymore. Turning to Arioch, she said to the demon, "You will obey me as when you obey the master. When we capture the wolf, he must be alive, and you will not beat him since he may die. The master needs him alive to bring the queen to her knees. They will all kneel before the master. Understand?"

Arioch looked at her, and she could tell he understood her command. Raven smiled and enchanted the demon. The last thing she needed was a human to recognize him in the car and cause any delay. When she finished her enchantment, a large, dark-haired man sat beside her, asleep. That was her signal to start driving in the direction that the raven flew.

Her mind wandered once again to the patriarch of her family. She tried to remember the stories of the man who bore the serpent's mark. She recalled the stories of Charlotte from her mother and grandmother. Charlotte was a powerful witch with the dark eye, or the sight, as it was referred to now. She could see the sins of a person's past or present by touching something that carried their scent. She remembered her mother telling her a story that was full of mystery.

The man with the serpent's mark appeared before Charlotte, and without saying a word, he held up his hand to her as if to give her a gift. Opening his hand, he revealed a small charm. Charlotte took the charm and smiled, thinking it was the most beautiful gift she had ever received. The man placed the charm on a string and tied it around her neck. Charlotte stopped smiling and gazed into his eyes.

"Wearing this charm will protect your soul. Through your darkness, a light shines true. A powerful witch will rise through your womb, breaking the bonds the master has cast. She will question her purpose but turn to the true witch of power in the hour of need. The raven and the light witch will battle like no other; their resolve lies

in the heart of power. Keep true to my words and guard this charm. In return, I will lay with you to begin the line. I hail from the line of Philip II, where the legend of the serpent begins. Should your line die before the raven witch is born, the master will collect the souls of the Hexham line."

The story always puzzled her every time she heard it, but thinking about it while she drove, something clicked inside her this time. Her foot pressed harder on the gas pedal without her paying attention, and she turned up the radio. She didn't want Arioch to hear her talk out loud. The story references a charm, but Charlotte has been dead for centuries, so what happened to it? Her mother kept a charm hidden in her jewelry chest, but that couldn't be the same charm, or could it?

Raven wasn't sure though curiosity clouded her intentions of finding the wolf. After she pulled over, she made sure Arioch wouldn't wake and cast another spell, this time to leave her body and go through her mother's house in secret. She opened the jewelry chest and saw the charm. She studied it carefully and turned the charm over and over without her projected form touching it, looking at its details and trying to sense its power. The charm suddenly turned green and began to glow. Raven had no choice but to return to her own body because she wasn't sure what the charm was doing. As she floated back into her body, she was out of breath but calmed herself. The demon didn't wake, so once she was in control of herself, she began driving in the same direction the raven had flown moments before she cast her spell.

***

Malakai, Delaware, 1990s

Malakai and Nikoli silently walked the area moments after being attacked by another pack of wolves. The two managed to defeat them all and left no survivors. Their shirts were in shreds, and their bodies were drenched with sweat, but Nikoli warned Malakai that they had to return to Miriam and the newborn.

As they walked, Malakai recalled the fight, and it was gruesome.

Before either man could change, Malakai and Nikoli found themselves surrounded by five wolves. He had felt these wolves were tracking them somehow, but a large black wolf started moving toward him. Saliva dripped from his fangs as the wolf prepared to pounce. Malakai knew this move all too well, and before the wolf could connect with him, he leaped into the air and changed into his wolf form. Malakai couldn't see what was happening to Nikoli, but telepathically, he urged him to change. The baby was just born, and he promised Miriam to bring her husband back to her. He could only hope that Nikoli had heeded his warning.

Malakai lunged for the black wolf, the one he assumed to be the alpha. His teeth sank into the neck of the alpha, and he could taste the sweetness of the blood. Once he felt the alpha's blood enter his throat, Malakai's eyes changed. The power from the blood flowed through his body, and he opened his jaws once more to take a deeper bite. The alpha's blood was calling to him as it flowed through his mouth. The alpha screamed in pain before dying.

Filled with rage and power, Malakai let out a howl so deep and powerful that it resembled those of the other alphas. He noticed Nikoli was fighting a wolf but had stopped, and he bowed to acknowledge Malakai's new role. The other wolves also bowed in reverence.

Malakai stood before them as a naked man, and spoke.

"I have the blood of your alpha coursing through my veins. You can bow to me now or walk away as rogues. My brother, Nikoli, stands among you. Harm him, a new

father, and you will bring about your death. Decide."

The wolves gave him their fealty, and Nikoli changed into a man. Nikoli rushed forward to embrace his brother and congratulate him on becoming an alpha of a pack.

Nikoli said, "Brother, I only wish you were the alpha of our pack. You are destined for such greatness."

Malakai smiled. "That is all but a formality. Let's see our pack's alpha and how we can merge the two. Maybe there is a way to accomplish all that you wish for. As for you wolves, change and follow us, and I will take you to meet the alpha."

Before Malakai and Nikoli could lead, the four wolves attacked them again. The men found the needed strength and killed the wolves, leaving a trail of blood. Nikoli and Malakai did not need to shift in order to kill the wolves.

When both faced the alpha, he wasn't interested in learning the truth, and he was more interested in the deaths of Nikoli and Malakai. Both men tried to tell him the truth of the attack and that Malakai had assumed rightful claim to the role of alpha by pack law. Furious, the alpha snapped at them.

"You will both die for killing betas that swore allegiance to you regardless. You will die because you decided to rise against your alpha's commands."

Malakai couldn't believe what he was hearing. *Against*

the alpha's commands? Again rage began to fester, and he felt the protective hand on his shoulder.

"Calm down, brother. Calm."

Through gritted teeth, Malakai's voice raged. "You planned to kill us? Nikoli and his mate just had a daughter and one that is destined for greatness. And you seek to kill us? An alpha goes against the law of the pack. Malakai, the wolf you embraced in your pack, now challenges you for the alpha role. This pack needs a leader who believes in pack law, not one who kills his own by hiring other packs or whatever you did."

Malakai didn't care about the alpha's ways anymore. He shifted and howled once more before striking his claw at the alpha. The alpha didn't move quickly enough, taking the slash across his face. Wolves came out from the bushes and those that were in human form started to make their way toward them. The wolves, mostly male, began to increase in numbers. Slowly, the whole pack made their way to see what happening with the alpha. By the time Malakai turned around, he saw the entire pack standing by the alpha though only half had shifted while the others remained human.

The other wolves then circled Malakai and the alpha, forcing the fight to happen. People were screaming, and the alpha shifted. Malakai's human side became dormant, and he called upon the blood of the fallen alpha inside his veins. A howl emerged that caused the others, including the alpha, to shiver. Malakai fought, knowing that Nikoli's baby girl's future was no longer possible if he was no longer the one standing. He had heard the alpha talk about killing the child before it got too late because of Nikoli's mate. Malakai made them both a promise to protect them and their daughter, no matter the cost. Finding his strength, he made a move against the alpha that proved to be his greatest sin. The alpha fell to his knees and breathed his last breath. He saw the other wolves submit in silence, calling him the alpha. Malakai never wanted to be an alpha, but something inside him changed.

"I will be your alpha one day. A privilege I hold sacred, but a duty and a promise before I can assume that role must be fulfilled. Till then, I need a right-hand man to lead you until I return. You have welcomed me into your pack, and I now ask you to pick a trustworthy man until I have fulfilled my promise to our brother Nikoli and his mate Miriam to protect their child—a child of our pack. Mark my words, my promise. I will return and be the alpha you need for justice, righteousness, and as one of the prophecy's faithful servants."

Clouds formed overhead, and the once-blue sky was now turning dark. Nikoli's eyes rolled backward and became white. Malakai could no longer see his pupils.

"From these lips, she speaks. I am the keeper of the prophecy. Till Malakai returns, honor the chosen one in his place as if you would honor Malakai, your alpha. His destiny and future lie in your survival. Seek out the dire wolves and merge packs. All will be known one day when the dark raven approaches."

Chapter Eleven
Danger

Kawika Kekahuna, Honolulu, Present Day

Kawika always listened to his grandfather, so he began researching events in the last five years in Seattle. He asked Malia to join him because she was the only one he trusted. Kawika searched the supernatural archives while Malia focused on the Seattle events. Both were quietly working on their own when Malia's scream brought Kawika back from daydreaming.

"Kawika, I found something! It's not a published article because nothing substantiated it. The person who took the notes is no longer alive, but a coven found it and kept the notes from the public. Strange, huh?"

Kawika headed towards her and started reading, more like skimming. The notes were about demons running around Seattle, and a young group of supernaturals was spotted around town: two vampires, a witch, and a red-headed woman. The notes didn't provide much detail, but the young people's names and the information was a few years old and still pretty recent.

Glad to have found something, Kawika said, "Continue searching for more clues. These must be the ones my grandfather spoke about. Find out anything you can."

Kawika went back to the archives to search for a woman called Illyris at one point. He didn't find much but came across other names. He just about gave up when he found an ancient text that caught his eye.

A warrior woman, mated to a cold one, sought an alliance with the wolf pack. The woman was strong and brave and is marked by a legend that stands against time. She has lived lifetimes, each with the same fate. Her mate seeks to kill her and the alliance to prevent the prophecy from happening.

The mark of the moon is found on her person and will glow when the prophecy needs her. To kill her will bring forth the destruction of the world. Each life she lives will be closer to her birthright, her chosen path. To find the warrior woman in any lifetime, call for her using the prophecy's words.

Kawika looked at the text and saw that rest of the page was missing, and there was no text about how to call this mysterious woman. Frustrated, he joined Malia in her search to see if there was more information about Seattle. After a few hours of reading various articles, they found one about the new talented employee of the largest museum in Seattle. She was gifted, graduated college at a young age, and was the most successful young curator in the museum's history. She had been promoted several times and worked closely with another talented woman deciphering ancient artifacts, especially Macedonian ones. The article even had a picture of a young woman, and one of them was a redhead. He studied the picture even more and saw something on her neck. It looked like a tattoo, but it was a crescent moon.

"Malia, this must be her! It fits the other text I read about a warrior woman long ago. Can you find anything out more about her?"

Malia looked at him with amazement and nodded.

"On it, Kawika. This is a lot more fun than our usual research. My tūtū said I should help you whenever you ask, and she said something about the power your family yields. Why didn't you tell me?"

"Malia! Focus! I will tell you of my family and the

line of kahunas that came before my grandfather. It is all tied together. I already know of your family and their power. I should ask… why didn't you tell me?" Kawika laughed at his joke, and eventually, Malia joined in.

Kawika was beginning to get one of his headaches again, and he started to feel nauseous. As his right hand reached his temple, his eyes began to roll back into his head. He could sense what was happening but couldn't see his surroundings or Malia.

In a voice not entirely his own, he said, "The queen is the one you seek, young kahuna. Seek and bring her to stand before the gods on Diamond Head. She must be here in one moon's time. Offer the gifts that please Pele and Kāne the most. Restore balance before the evil one returns once more. As they helped the evil one, they will help you."

When Kawika's senses returned, Malia was busy scribbling down what had just happened. He reached for her notes, and she began to read them to him instead. After she was finished, he asked Malia to find Amber's address.

"She's the one we need. Let's ask her to come."

Malia went on the internet to look for a recent address. Kawika began to prepare a letter for the young woman. He had hoped she would be the key to all this. He struggled to find the words, but as he said his family prayer, the pen began writing as if it knew his thoughts. When he was done, he assembled a package to bring this woman to the islands.

***

Nimue, The Dark Forest, Present Day

Nimue led the others through the forest, following the path that revealed itself to her. She remained focused on the task ahead, but something was talking to her – from inside her head. At first, it started as whispers, but the voice grew louder.

"My sweet Nimue. Did you think I would be a fool to let you go so easily? Foolish girl."

Nimue covered her ears and fell to her knees. Tears rolled down her cheeks as she tried to fight the voice in her head. It was him, and he found her again. Nimue closed her eyes as tight as she could and put more pressure on covering her ears. She felt gentle hands on her shoulders as she remained on the ground.

She opened her eyes, expecting to see him, but instead, she looked right into McPherson's eyes.

"McPherson, it's you. Really you. He found me again,

and he's in my head, and I can't get him to stop."

"Who? Tell me, Nimue. Don't be afraid. Better yet, can I touch you to see for myself?"

Nimue choked back a tear and nodded. McPherson removed his glove and placed his fingers across her temple. She could hear him mumble a few words but couldn't quite make out what he was saying. The pain grew in her head, and she screamed.

McPherson pulled his hand back and held it tight against his chest. She watched him and saw why he did so. His hand was blistered, and though he didn't scream, she knew the Tall Dark Man had done this to her friend. McPherson sat on the ground, cradling his blistered hand and cursing a storm.

Gathering her courage, Nimue stood on her own once again. Raising her hands to the sky, she began to weave and chant to him.

"Master of the Darkness, Master of the Wasteland, I call you to stand before me. Not your true form, but your shadow. Come forth and face me."

As she waited for him to appear, she noticed the fear in McPherson's eyes.

"Nimue, what have you done? We are exposed here. Don't be daft, girl."

Nimue waved his protests away. Suddenly, the Tall

Dark Man appeared. In front of her as she commanded through her spell. The Tall Dark Man's shadow had answered her call.

Trying to hide her own fear, Nimue said, "Unbind me, master. I no longer serve you but serve another. Set my soul free."

The Tall Dark Man's shadow laughed at her, taunting her foolish wishes, and said, "I will unbind you when the angel is mine, her father is mine, and the queen is dead. Till then, I will see through your eyes, hear through your ears; I will know everything that comes before you. You are mine till then."

Nimue screamed in horror. Her fears were coming true, and she was still in his service. Everything she had been working towards – helping to save her best friend, learning from McPherson, and wanting to be helpful to Amber – was up in flames because of him.

McPherson tried to speak, but Rowe's voice was the one she heard.

"You are not alone, Nimue. We know what's in your heart now by all your actions. The Tall Dark Man will not win. Trust in McPherson. Please."

McPherson finally said, "You are not his servant. But you will be if you believe his words. We must continue, regardless of what he says. We need the totem. Nimue, be strong. Zaraquel is counting on you."

Nimue wiped her tears and thought of her friend. She forged on, knowing that he was watching her and could see and hear everything now that they would endure. As she walked on, she tried to figure out how to prevent him from stopping them. Nimue was more determined than ever to destroy the Tall Dark Man.

***

The Tall Dark Man, Underground, Present Day

He sat on his throne, watching the coven of witches continuing to create his army. He was bored, and Raven wasn't there; his witch Elizabeth was recovering, and his Tituba again proved loyal to him. The Tall Dark Man wanted to see his concubine witch carry this particular child to fruition. Moving along the corridor, he stopped just outside his study. As he listened to the quiet of his underground lair, he smiled and opened the door.

"Parchments of ancient times, bring the words to my lips that will guide my witch Tituba to deliver a child faster than before."

The parchments began to move around the table, dropping to the floor, and one began to glow. As it caught his attention, a flame erupted in the corner. The parchment wasn't burning but signaling him to read it. The Tall Dark Man reached for the parchment and began to read its writing. His eyes narrowed as he read the text, and his mouth tightened. He thought *I could bring back a more powerful hunter through Tituba if I followed this ancient text. I wonder if it would work. All I have to do is sacrifice one witch in my service with enough power for Tituba. But which one? I would never harm Elizabeth or Raven; they are both too powerful and loyal to him. There must be another.*

The Tall Dark Man consulted the book of witches in his possession. This book contained the names of all witches in the world, light or dark. Page after page, he ran his finger down the list of names. Then he saw the one that stood out. Perfect. He found the witch to sacrifice and loved his plan for vengeance even more than before. All he needed to do was ensure Arioch and Raven followed through on their task to bring the wolf to him, and then the rest would come to him, including the witch he needed to sacrifice.

***

Marcus, The Estate, Present Day

The three of them were back at the estate in the

library, watching as Marcus instructed Amber to open the book. Jerome was tending to Marcus' magical reminder of his agreement with the Tall Dark Man. As Jerome finished, he gathered up the ointments and bowed to Amber as he left the library, but not before telling them to call for him if his services were needed again.

Still wincing from the pain, Marcus said, "Amber, turn to the page with a blood moon in the top right corner. Not all pages are marked, so use a spell if necessary. The blood moon was the symbol both Michael and Kabos came up with to mark certain pages that we all studied."

Amber whispered her spell, and they all watched as the pages flipped. Marcus held his breath, hoping her spell was strong enough for this book. He recalled that Michael had once enchanted this book because of its secrets, and there were times he just wasn't himself. Michael had confided to him long ago about the Stone of the Damned and how it destroyed him, causing him to lose himself to evil. Still, one thing was clear – Michael was more powerful than the Stone but not robust enough to guard himself against keeping from becoming Machiel again.

The book stopped and remained open on the page. Marcus saw the blood moon in the top right corner and said, "This is the page! Let me read it unless you want to try it, Amber. The book is now yours."

"I'll try. Let's see what is written."

> *When the blood moon rises, a child will rise to the be scepter of the queen during her unification. The child will grow in the ways of the light, but when she is no longer a child, she will fall into the arms of the Dark One, the one marked by a goat. Her soul will be at a crossroads until she drinks the blood of the alpha wolf to whom she is linked upon birth.*
>
> *Should she not drink, the Dark One will capture her soul, and she will be lost to the queen forever. The queen will then fall should she lose her scepter. The bonds of blood between the witch and the cold one will also fade, and evil will run rampant through the world, ceasing the Blood Prophecy and giving birth to the Prophecy of Darkness.*

Amber stopped reading and looked toward Marcus, seeking more knowledge of what Michael had left for her. Marcus turned and looked at Chloe, whose face looked as if she had seen a ghost. Marcus remembered this page, but never did he think that this would come true, but there they were, and the possibilities seemed too natural that this might be the end of his daughter and evil would rule the world. Marcus couldn't let himself get distracted. He needed Malakai here, but something told him that the alpha wolf wasn't returning home for some time. Frustrated, he yelled to the air, even though his wife and the queen were before him.

"FUCK! Where is that damned stone? That stone is what he'd be after. Michael told me that the Tall Dark Man wanted Michael to give it to him willingly, but he refused in the beginning when he first received the stone. Let's see if I can remember what he told me. Give me a minute to think."

The room was silent and then Marcus spoke once more.

"It was centuries ago when he was still Machiel. He and Kabos travelled together but he was so resentful to Kabos about the prophecy but only because he couldn't understand his role to accept it. He told me that that the Tall Dark Man showed himself as a little boy in a forest and tried to tempt him in order to get the stone. Machiel was given a choice later and he chose to accept the stone. The rest I can't recall. But the whole thing about the Tall Dark Man being more powerful now pisses me off."

Marcus then began to throw books from the shelves and leaped to the desk. With one arm swipe, he moved all the items on the desk to the floor. The bottom broke loose as a lamp hit the floor, revealing a key hidden in the lamp's base. Neither woman noticed and they did not make a move. He realized his anger scared Chloe.

Ignoring the pain in his hand, Marcus said, "It's a key. Amber, come. Bring the book. Please. And Chloe, I'm sorry. Michael was a man of mystery, and our life was so complicated, but to learn that there was a Dark Prophecy was the last thing I wanted to hear. I never meant to put Zara in any harm, and I wanted her to be happy again."

Marcus broke down into tears. Amber came closer and picked up the key. She took the lamp and started examining the bottom. As her hands felt the secret compartment, a piece of paper fell out. She opened it and read it aloud.

> *Mí Amor, Marcus, and Chloe. If you find this key, you will need to find the stone. The Stone of the Damned is hidden in this house. Follow the clues and pay attention to what they are because all is lost if this falls into The Tall Dark Man's hands. My body couldn't hold onto the stone after losing, so Jerome hid it but kept it close to me. It will*

take you three to figure out where he has hidden this stone when things got worse for me.

1.   Marcus – What year did Kabos welcome you into our family? Those are the number of paces from the back door heading east.
2.   Amber – From where you stand after walking out the back door, head to the north by stopping at the two trees where we talked about our future, and you told me about your childhood.
3.   Chloe – The year your ancestor died in Salem. The one whom the Witch Prophecy begins with. From Amber's place, walk those paces, and once you arrive, use your ability to release the stone from the earth. An ordinary shovel will not suffice.
These are cryptic for a reason. The Stone of the Damned connects to the Tall Dark Man. Marcus, my beloved son, you were given to me by Kabos so that I could learn to be a maker, a father, and a friend. Though I did not sire you, we both understood the

bonds that tie us. I must ask you, Marcus. The stone must remain in the enchanted cloth. The Romani gypsies, Kabos' birth family, and what remains of them, consecrated it to shield it.

Seek the dire wolves – the guardians of the prophecy. Sabre will know how to find the White Wolf named Keela. I hope for our sake she is still alive. It's been centuries, but as a guardian, she would live unless evil has taken her last breath. She will know how to guide you as I cannot fulfill the destiny placed in my hands when I accepted the stone and the book.

*Now, **Mí Amor**. For the words I could not say when I was with you. I am sorry for our loss in love, my failure against the king, and for betraying you and the prophecy.*

Always and forever,
Michael

After Marcus listened to his father's words, he became engrossed with emotion and purpose. He whispered to the library as if the room had Michael's spirit. "I accept the Stone of the Damned into my care and destiny. I will do your will, father."

Gathering his courage, he encouraged Amber and Chloe to follow the letter's instructions. He wouldn't dig up the stone yet, but he wanted to know the location so that when they were ready, they could obtain this cursed stone and protect it from the Tall Dark Man.

***

Sabre, Seattle, Present Day

Sabre sped along the highway for at least an hour before he had reception. Immediately, he placed a call to Marcus.

"Come on, pickup, vampire. Pickup!" Sabre said in a low tone.

Marcus answered his phone. Sabre didn't wait for him to say hello before he began rambling about Malakai and the curse.

Marcus finally managed to interject, "Whoa, slow down, brother. Say again? Is Malakai on all fours? McPherson is on a quest. He should be reachable since he took his satellite phone so we can stay in contact. I'll send you the number. The queen and Chloe are busy with another task, but I can come to you if you need me. We will find McPherson ourselves."

Sabre was quiet for a moment. His pack had always been loyal to Michael and Kabos since they met Killen, one of its ancient elders, who had long since passed. The stories of Killen were always shared with the pack's young members so they would learn the code of protection for Michael, Kabos, and the rest. Killen died a long time ago protecting his mate, but the sacrifices he made for the pack's future and the alliance he made with Michael, once known as Machiel, brought them all to the queen and her victory over The Tall Dark Man.

Marcus' voice brought him back from his reminiscing. "Sabre. Brother. Did I lose you? Damn reception."

"No, I'm still here. I was thinking about Michael and an old story about him and our pack. Send me McPherson's number. I'm going to stop at an exit for Snoqualmie Pass. There's an all-night diner. Find me there, and we will look for the wizard. Tell the queen about our plans so that she remains protected. I can send two dire wolves to protect her, but the rest must watch over Malakai."

"Got it, but she's in good hands with Chloe and the others here. Let's see if I can beat you there, brother."

Within seconds after disconnecting, his cell beeped, alerting him to a text. Using Bluetooth features in his car, he managed to call the number Marcus gave him, and he just let it ring, hoping McPherson would pick up. After a few minutes, the phone connected. McPherson answered, but Sabre could barely hear over the static.

"This is McPherson. Lots of static because of where I am. Who is calling, please?"

"I'll be quick. This is Sabre. Marcus and I need to find you. Things are happening. Malakai is cursed; the queen may be in danger because of the curse. Give me your coordinates."

McPherson was silent, but Sabre could hear him mumbling something to other people. Finally, he returned and gave Sabre the coordinates before telling him it was in a Dark Forest, but he would cast a spell to guide them. He just needed to know where he and Marcus would be. Sabre told him the diner's location, and they'd be there in a couple of hours before disconnecting. Then he stepped on the gas while he let out a loud howl, hoping that Black Wind would hear the howl.

Finally, Sabre reached the diner and found Marcus already inside. The wolf chuckled before going inside. Somehow Sabre knew that evil was brewing, but it wasn't just focused on the queen and her friends, it was more, and he didn't know how much more.

Chapter Twelve
Oceans Across

Zaraquel, The Witch's Cottage, Present Day

Zaraquel continued to work with Garnet Rose, using all the magic she could muster, to form her demon in her likeness. Not physical likeness but everything she wanted in a demon to help her on her journey. She knew she would have to keep Garnet Rose hidden so the witch wouldn't discover what she had created alone. The deception was vital. Zaraquel knew she had to stay to master the dark magic, but learning that the Tall Dark Man was coming for her made her tremble with fear. Garnet Rose must've sensed her fear because before she knew it, her demon threw her on the ground and stood over her in a protective stance.

She spoke to the demon with her mind, hoping this would work so the witch wouldn't discover them.

"Garnet Rose, I'm safe. Get off me. I need to hide you someplace safe, but I want you to protect me if the witch does something bad. Got it?"

Garnet Rose twisted her head as if she understood. With a slight nod, Zaraquel knew her demon understood her.

"I need you to hide. Go to my room and stay there. I must call the witch for my lessons. Protect me at all costs. I gave you many powers that will protect you from the witch. I also gave you memories of the queen and my parents to help you if I am ever in danger. You would listen to them as you would to me. Go now."

Once she knew the demon was safely away, Zaraquel started making noise and calling for the witch. It was time to return to her lessons despite what she knew about the Tall Dark Man. Anne was prepared to teach her, but Zaraquel was distracted by the words of the Tall Dark Man.

"Practice, angel," Anne said. "You must create a demon, and we are losing time. Do it now."

Zaraquel began to create another demon following the witch's commands exactly. After some time, a solid demon was standing before her, but it was just a shell. Something was wrong. Her demon wasn't alive, at least not for her. She could see that Anne was losing her patience, but she was determined to find a way to do all but not be in the hands of evil. Zaraquel missed her mother and father.

Anne was about to slap Zaraquel, or so she thought, before a knock on the door prevented Anne from doing anything to her. Lowering her hand, Anne mumbled something inaudible. The door opened, and it looked like another witch. Anne must've realized the other witch's power because she bowed before the witch. The witch strolled in with an attitude, and Zaraquel was afraid as the newcomer said, "Is this the angel the master wants to be prepared? She looks rather young for all that power she possesses. How old are you, angel?"

Zaraquel gulped and tried to hold her ground. "I'm an adult and look young because of… my nature. Who are you?"

"I am Elizabeth Hexham. Surely, you remember me, angel?"

Zaraquel didn't remember, but inside her mind, she felt something calling her. She couldn't make out who or what it was, but it was a feeling she couldn't shake. A voice spoke in her head.

"Zara, I won't harm you. I once loved you. Remember whose daughter you are! I am not in HIS service anymore."

She knew that voice, but it couldn't be. Loquiel. She

ended things with him years ago. But why would he help her? Then the words struck true. REMEMBER WHOSE DAUGHTER YOU ARE! Her wings began to burn. A little red showed, but the rest was growing darker.

Clenching her teeth, she screamed.

"I AM THE DAUGHTER OF THE LIGHT WITCH AND A VAMPIRE. I AM THE AVENGING ANGEL, AND I WILL MASTER THE DARK MAGIC, BUT IT WILL NOT MASTER ME!"

A red light emerged from her hands and directly impacted Elizabeth Hexham. The witch screamed. Zaraquel collapsed on the ground, breathing heavily, but noticed that Elizabeth Hexham was nowhere to be seen. Where did the bitch go? She was tired, but as she hoisted herself onto her elbows, she stared down the witch.

"Anne," Zaraquel said as she caught her breath, "you will teach me, and then I will let you live. Your bargain was with my father, not the Tall Dark Man. Do you hear me?"

Anne was not scared, but she just nodded in acquiescence. "I hear you, angel, but there's not much time. Letting me put you in a light slumber would be best. Will you let me? You won't master the dark while you battle whatever is inside you."

Zaraquel nodded. After all, she had heard, she wasn't

sure if she should trust this witch now, but she was so close. Anne smiled eerily at her, but Zaraquel didn't feel good about it. The last thing she heard was Anne saying, "Sleep."

*****

King Kamehameha, Niihau, "The Forbidden Island", 1810

Niihau was always under the ruler of the ali'i, the highest ruling class in the islands. Despite the numerous attempts made by King Kamehameha, he was unable to unite the island with the rest. This did not sit well with him. Each failed attempt left him with more bloodshed and tears and his warriors were now part of the Night Marchers. Night Marchers were something he could not control.

Even before another bloody battle would take place, King Kamehameha was visited by none other than the supreme ruler, Kaumuali'i. Kaumuali'i was the last ruling monarch of Niihau and Kauai, the two territories he sought to unite.

"Aloha au I ko'u po'e. Make ko kakou mau koa ke kaua kakou. Ke lawe 'o Kāne i ko'u ola, e noho ali'i kou ho'oilina iā Kauai ma hope o'u."

King Kamehameha thought long and hard about this ali'i's offer of peace. His heir would rule after Kaumuali'i's death, which would sit well with him, but what of the night marchers? Would they accept this peace between the islands? King Kamehameha responded to the ali'i.

"No ko kakou poe." For our people. He would agree if both prayed to the gods to control the night marchers. King Kamehameha knew that the night marchers preyed on bloodshed, but there would be no more beginning this night. In his eyes, the rulers united the Hawaiian people.

Later that night, the two united rulers prayed to the gods reverently, but Kū, the god of War, appeared before them. Kū was angry at the two rulers.
"I kēlā me kēia makahiki e ho'ohanohano 'oe ia'u me ke kaua koko."

Ku demanded that the rulers have a bloody battle once a year in exchange for peace. Both rulers had no choice but to agree to show Kū their respect—one battle of blood a year for a lifetime of peace. Kamehameha thought later that night that the battle demanded would only be a short battle between two men. He wanted peace more than anything for the Hawaiian people. And he finally managed to get Kaumuali'i to accept his rule and unification of the Hawaiian Islands. As he slept that night, visions of a woman warrior saving his people entered his mind. *Who is this woman?*

***

Tituba, Underground, Present Day

Tituba was cradling her stomach while wincing in pain. She had never experienced such pain before when she carried the master's seeds. She closed her eyes and prayed that the seed would not be lost again. Tituba couldn't imagine her life without the Tall Dark Man and the witches she befriended over the centuries. She heard footsteps and barely turned her head when she heard his voice.

"Rise, Tituba. You are dressed lovely, but we have a short ceremony to perform to speed up your pregnancy. Come here."

As he motioned toward her with one finger, his other hand dragged something from behind and flung it at her feet. Looking down, it was one of the witches, but she didn't recognize her. The witch on the floor didn't even flinch.

Confused, Tituba asked, "What's this, master? The hunter is growing inside me."

The Tall Dark Man flashed one of his sinister smiles.

Tituba always thought him handsome, but this time, he looked different.

He said, "We will ensure the hunter's arrival. My plan is coming together faster than anticipated but is incomplete without the hunter. You will kill this witch and absorb her power immediately. She is a strong witch, and you need her power. Do it. I will watch."

The witch's eyes grew wide at the words of the Tall Dark Man, and she looked at Tituba. Tituba was suddenly feeling powerful and hungry for power, and these feelings were not coming directly from her. She closed her eyes and tried to connect with the child growing inside her despite it being only a short time since the Tall Dark Man planted his seed.

"Child, is this power yours? How can that be?" She whispered silently to herself.

The hunter made a slight movement in response. Tituba wasn't sure if it was him or just something she imagined. She knew she had no choice but to obey the master. Reaching down to grab the witch by the hand, she smiled and said, "We must obey the master. I am Tituba. And have you come willingly to serve the master and offer your power to me?"

The witch nodded. "I am of service to my lord and master."

With a nod, Tituba removed a blade she always kept attached to her leg and drew a pentagram on the witch's forehead. Blood began to trickle down her face. Tituba began to wave her hands around and chant. She called for the witch's power to be absorbed into her, not the hunter's. She needed this power.

Inside, her body was screaming with the surge of power from the witch. As the heat intensified, her body began to burn from the inside out. She felt like she was on fire amid the transfer. The witch slowly lost her power while blood trickled down her forehead. Tituba was growing stronger. Her womb began to ache with a pang of hunger. She closed her eyes and tried to control the twitching by letting her power combine with the incoming power. Once the merge was complete, Tituba knew the next step. Taking her blade in one hand, she walked around to the back of the witch. Grabbing her hair by the roots, she tilted the witch's head back, exposing the neck. Tituba angled the blade and cut across the throat, letting her blood spill forward. The witch made no attempts to resist and accepted her role as the sacrifice to obey the Tall Dark Man.

The Tall Dark Man smiled and began to say the spell. Tituba began to feel strange and protectively cradled her womb like any mother would. She felt the hunter stir, and a voice spoke in her head.

"Hear my voice, mother? I am the hunter - the bringer of death, the demon of destruction, and the voice of all evil. You will love me like no other, but I will drink your blood upon my birth. I will cause you pain like no other. Before you wither into nothingness, my eyes will be the last thing you shall see."

Tituba couldn't believe what she had just heard and looked at the Tall Dark Man with utter confusion. He smiled at her, touching her womb to feel the hunter inside, and said, "You've outworn your usefulness to me except for this birth. Failure to deliver my hunter will only cause you pain."

Tituba didn't want to die, and she needed to choose. She remembered what Raven had said to her. *Think, Tituba, think.*

"Master, if you are displeased with all the demons I brought forth for your will, then I am not worthy. Yet you always seemed pleased with my demon children. Perhaps you and I can come to another arrangement?"

She ran her dark finger against the master's cheek. She let her mouth open as if to kiss him. Tituba pulled him into her while letting her other hand stroke his member. She knew how to lure men ever since she was a child. The witch trials only enhanced her knowledge, and being trapped with him here made her wiser to seducing him easily. Before she knew it, she trapped the Tall Dark Man in her embrace of seduction. His body moved alongside hers in intense fervor without him realizing the spell she was casting on him. Before she could finish her entrapment, the door flew open, and it was Elizabeth Hexham. Tituba tried to finish but was instantly frozen by Elizabeth's spell.

As Tituba fought against the magic, Elizabeth said, "Sammael, release yourself from her embrace. NOW! Tituba was entrancing you, and I could feel you becoming trapped."

The Tall Dark Man ignored Elizabeth's command. He was lost to Tituba. Elizabeth rushed forward and threw him off of her. Tituba couldn't respond, only glare at her. The Tall Dark Man shook his head as if confused. Elizabeth repeated herself and freed him from the magic embrace. The Tall Dark Man began to snarl at Tituba, realizing what she had done.

"Foolish witch! You will bear my hunter, and then I will feed you to my demons. Your service to me ends after you birth my hunter. My Elizabeth, I am grateful for your connection to me. I knew it would one day serve me well. And it has. Take me away from here, my favorite witch. I need to gain my strength."

As he tried to stand, he couldn't. Eventually, Elizabeth helped him, leaving Tituba alone and frozen in her spot.

Tituba would find a way to free herself.

***

Amber, Seattle Museum, Present Day

Amber was working her usual night hours, trying to focus, when her assistant Kimberly knocked on her door and carried a large package labeled "FRAGILE, HANDLE WITH CARE" on the sides. Amber wrinkled her nose with interest, and no matter how much people revered her genius or the fact that she was the vampire queen, she loved mysteries.

Once her assistant left her alone with the package, she eagerly grabbed it and flew to the other side of the room. Letting her claws extend, she cut through the tape quickly, and a letter was inside.

> *Aloha Queen,*
> *I am Kawika Kekahuna, a descendant of*
> *the great Kahunas in the islands of Hawai'i.*
> *We require your help to stop evil from*
> *taking over our islands. I am not a man of*
> *too many words, so in this box are a few*
> *more pieces you can display with the other*

artifacts from our islands. Have the witch touch them; if what she sees intrigues her, you will find the tickets in this box for your travels. You would be traveling under special arrangements to show I understand your nature. I wouldn't be so vague if I knew whom I could trust. Our islands and the people need you to help me save us from evil. Though I am from a great line of Kahunas, words you may not understand, I am just as you and your friends are with special powers, if you understand my meaning.

Mahalo,
Kawika Kekahuna

Amber sorted through the box and was more intrigued by this. She had always wanted to travel the world and got a little teary-eyed remembering the conversations with Michael. She immediately called for Chloe to come to her office. The benefits of their friendship and Malakai being their boss allowed Amber and Chloe to work nights.

When Chloe arrived, Amber said, "Chloe, reach into the box. I didn't touch anything yet. Touch them and tell me what you see."

Chloe looked at her as if she had lost her damn mind. Amber just laughed because she could always tell what she was thinking. "Just do it."

Shrugging her shoulders, Chloe reached into the box and lifted the first statue. Her fingers ran over the face, the crevices, the back, the bottom. She closed her eyes while she did this and said, "I see four spirits, and they look like spirits. They are on a volcano or something near a fire pit, and I see them looking at the water. I think it is a place where the other exhibits come from. Tropical, ancient."

"Good, keep going." Amber was anxious.

Chloe grabbed another statue. "Same thing. But there's a wizard or something. Someone like McPherson. He has power, and he's fighting a group of ghosts or something like that. It's giving me a strong vibe about a battle. There's another item in here. Let me try that one."

Chloe reached into the box and removed a rather ordinary-looking rock. After she studied it, it was just a regular rock. She closed her eyes to do her stuff, and Amber watched her closely as she said, "I see a man near a beach. It doesn't look too far in the past, more like recent. I usually don't see visions of current situations. Amber, he has an aura around him. I sense he's a witch or something. He has powers, and he is protected by something. I can't sense what, however. Amber, this is crazy. What the fuck is all this stuff for?"

Amber smiled, trying to reassure her friend, but she couldn't.

"I think this is due to the voice I heard from your lips the other day. I'm talking about volcanoes and shit. Then I got this package. I think this is where we need to go. I'm unsure if I go alone or if we all go. I wish Malakai were here, but lately, I've been thinking more and more about Michael. Can you reach Marcus?"

"I'll try. Let's first see what else is in the box."

Chloe rummaged through the box and held up two tickets. Amber took them and studied them—one for her and one for Chloe.

Amber grinned and said, "Looks like it's just you and me. We leave in about a month. Chloe – I'm not so sure about this. Are we being separated from the others when the Tall Dark Man is back? We need to explore more in the library. Let's see what Michael was really up to."

Amber and Chloe headed back to the estate and decided to bring Jerome up to speed on what they'd discovered. She wasn't sure how this fit in with the Tall Dark Man because it took her, Zaraquel, and everyone else to defeat him in the last battle years ago. And that was after she had died at Michael's hand, and she was only alive because of Zaraquel. As she thought about the Tall Dark Man being back, her crescent birthmark began to glow and burn as if it were telling her something. The heat from the mark became so intense that her skin was burning.

She screamed at the excruciating burning, and the smell got to her. Her scream must've pierced Chloe's ears because she fell to her knees, covering them. Amber fell to the ground due to the pain, and a voice spoke to her.

"The wolves will lay down their lives for you. Will you lay down your life for his? Bring him to me if you want him in his human form. In three days, I will contact you again. If you refuse, I will send the master's latest demon to devour everything in your cute estate, including your old butler. By the way, the witch must hide her book of shadows better. It was easy to find."

Amber rose to her feet, fangs bared, and began to snarl. She felt like howling, given her wolf genes, but she refused to let that voice know where she was. Instead, she helped Chloe and fled to the estate.

Chapter Thirteen
Balance

Nimue, The Dark Forest, Present Day

Nimue followed the path, but the words lingered in her head. *HE sees through my eyes, listening to what I say to help my friends; he will know my every move. Our every move. Looking towards the trees, she wondered if he could see what she saw. What if I talked to him?*

Rowe interrupted her thoughts when he asked, "Nimue, do you remember our time in Camelot? That one day when you froze me and stole the necklace. Do you remember the curse that you lay on me?"

She thought for a moment. "I... I think so. Do you want me to curse you again? When you're a ghost?"

"No. Think about whom you want to curse now and change the words. You have that power in you. Don't let him win now."

"I don't know if I can, but I will try in a bit. We must find that totem for McPherson, and it has to be nearby because the two totems must balance each other. Let's keep going."

She could see that something was wrong with McPherson. He was not moving as fast, and he was looking pale. She knew he had stopped to answer a call, but this was different. Turning to him, she stared directly at him. Nimue even forgot that the Tall Dark Man was still inside her.

"McPherson, what's wrong?"

McPherson coughed but then replied. "Sabre and Marcus are on their way. Malakai is a wolf, Zaraquel is in danger, and this evil force is too powerful. I cast a spell to guide them to our location, but my life is draining. I think it's because of this totem. A living person is not meant to hold it. We need Marcus."

Then he collapsed to the ground.

Nimue tried hard to remember what her new family had been teaching her. She struggled with the memories, especially considering what the Tall Dark Man had said to her moments before. Looking around for Rowe and Kabos, she no longer saw their spirits. *Where the hell did they go now?* She was alone with McPherson and, in a way, the Tall Dark Man. He was getting to her. This was one of his mind tricks. He might not even be here with her. Then again, he was the evil one. Nimue thought she was going crazy.

She sat on the ground near McPherson, and he was still breathing. Closing her eyes, she summoned her power. She knew she couldn't call Zaraquel and wasn't in the mood to piss off Amber. The one she needed most was Chloe. Nimue slowed down her breathing and focused on Chloe. Remembering everything that Merlin, well, Rowe now, taught her, she whispered her name.

"Chloe. Chloe. Hear my call, witch of the light. Witch of the power I seek. I call upon you, witch of the greatest power in the world. Speak to me."

She opened her eyes and waited. Nothing happened. She repeated her call once more. This time, a ball of light came directly at her in the dark of night. It threw her onto the earth and floated above her. Her head was hurting from this magic ball.

Nimue smiled as the light responded to Chloe's voice, "I hear you, Nimue. You're calling me. Why?"

"I need you, Chloe. Everything is wrong. McPherson is dying. I think he's dying. We need Marcus. The Tall Dark Man won't let me go. We have one totem, but we need the other. Only Marcus can hold the totem that is killing McPherson. This is all my fault. I failed." She started sobbing.

"Nimue, you are not failing. Magic comes at a price. The Tall Dark Man's hold on you will not be the reason you fail. You are stronger than you think. Trust in your teacher. Rowe will not lose you to him. We all won't. I can't leave Amber, but I can send you a special gift if you accept it. Will you trust me, little witch?"

"I trust you, Chloe. What is this gift?"

The ball of light shook slightly as Nimue could hear Chloe laugh and say, "She's a part of me, and I think you'll like her."

The ball disappeared, and, next to her, stood a white tiger, majestic and calm as Nimue gave a quick little shudder. *Don't be afraid, Nimue. Don't be afraid.* The tiger made a large sound that shook the dark forest before it nuzzled her nose into Nimue's shoulder. She held out her hand towards the tiger to let her sniff it. The tiger was enormous, much larger than any she had seen before. It wasn't quite the large size of a dire wolf but more significant than most wild cats. The tiger sniffed at McPherson's body, trying to nudge him. Nimue wondered how this *gift* was to help her while they waited for Sabre and Marcus to arrive.

Then she saw it. The tiger kept shaking McPherson until something rolled out of his pack—the wrapped totem. The tiger picked it up in its mouth, and

McPherson began to stir.

Before she could process everything, Nimue blurted out, "Holy shit!"

The tiger was carrying the totem of death in its mouth, and McPherson slowly stood on his feet. He was groggy and weak, but he was alive! Nimue felt better with Chloe's idea of a gift to help her until his voice spoke to her again.

"Foolish witch. I see the tiger; I see all. Bring them to me, including the wizard, the tiger, all. Do as I command, or I will remind you of your obedience to me."

Her head began to throb in intense pain, and Nimue fell to her knees. She tried to resist the pain and stand up, but a force kept her down. He was waiting for her to acquiesce to his will. Nimue screamed. This time she screamed for Marcus. The Tall Dark Man kept a tight hold on her, trying to force her to submit through momentary episodes of pain. The pain gripped her like nothing she felt before. All parts of her body felt like thousands of pins were piercing her at the same time, and then it would stop for a moment before starting again. The next pain was excruciating. From her knees, she fell over into a fetal position and screamed even louder.

Having finally collapsed, Nimue lost her will to keep resisting, and all she could think about was her new life.

Her path to redemption was disappearing before her eyes.

***

Anne Koldings, The Witch's Cottage, Present Day

Anne welcomed the Tall Dark Man into the cottage. She was not expecting him so soon, but he was anxious to see his angel. She managed to subdue Zaraquel by deceiving her. Anne told her that the master wanted to teach her the darkest spells that would be the last lessons she needed. Her goal was to erase her memory of the Tall Dark Man's visit so that she could continue with his plan to prepare her.

"Bring her to me."

"Master, you must go to her. I put her in a light slumber to allow her wings to darken more without her being conflicted. There are times when her light magic is still strong, and I plan to speed up the influence of the darkness while she sleeps. With your permission, of course."

"Take me to her. Now. We will discuss my plans for her when I have seen her."

Anne brought him to her and watched from a distance.

The Tall Dark Man studied the angel, touching her wings, and then placed his fingers on her forehead. "*Ostende mihi te.*"

Anne started to leave the room, knowing the master would want privacy for whatever he was about to see, but he said, "Stay. Witness."

She reached for his arm, knowing that touching him would allow her to witness what he would see. Anne knew better than to speak. Then she saw what he saw.

Zaraquel and Nimue laughing and talking. Hugging. Zaraquel and her mother are fighting. Then her father appears. The angel is crying in the arms of her father. Zaraquel embraces the dark magic, yet the wings still show a touch of red.

"Enough." The Tall Dark Man released his spell from the angel and said, "She still has too much light in her. Anne, Mother of the Devil, I command you to speed this up. She needs to be mine. There is another prophecy and one I just learned. Let's talk. She sleeps, but she can hear."

Anne showed him to the other side of the cottage. "Sit, master. Talk to me."

The Tall Dark Man removed his coat and hat before sitting down. Anne always thought him a handsome man, despite his scars. He was thinking about something that kept him distracted.

"There is a darker prophecy and an ancient parchment in my possession tells of a way for my vengeance to prosper. I can undo the queen and her victory from the second prophecy by making the angel my bride, my consort. She will birth the greatest of all demons that will unleash the reckoning of the queen. Tituba will give birth to the hunter that will destroy them all. And I will unite all the stones once more to set things in motion. I will prevail and destroy all that the Fates were trying to protect. I will win over the queen, and to hell with the blood prophecy this time. The dark prophecy will inherit the world, and all my demons will rise to fulfill its will, beginning with the hunter."

"Master, you always talk about this hunter. Who is this hunter?"

Anne was careful not to anger him, but she wanted to know what would happen to her because she was the Mother of the Devil. Anne lingered her finger over his shoulder, massaged his shoulders, and whispered in his ear, "Have I displeased you in any way that you don't seek to plant your seed in me?"

"You can only displease me if you fail with the angel. Your role in this is vital to my plan. Without you, my plan will not succeed. Turn her. Quickly."

Anne bowed to him in fealty to his favor. She would

succeed for him.

"I will turn her. She will favor you, master. But what of the hunter? Who is he?"

The master smiled. "All I need is Tituba to birth him. Then I will have no more use for her. She betrays me with every breath she takes. She was the only suitable witch to bear him next to you. I need you to handle this delicate situation in the other room. This angel's value is higher than the hunter is to me. Turn her. She must no longer be connected to the blood prophecy. I need her to be mine. All mine."

"Understood, master. Shall I take care of your other needs, or are you needed elsewhere?"

"I've recovered from that bitch Tituba. See to my needs."

***

Marcus, Diner, Present Day

Marcus was already waiting for Sabre, worried the wolf would not appear before sunrise. He managed to contact Chloe to let her know what was happening but was interrupted when she informed him of the package and the request for her and Amber to visit Hawaii to help them with a problem. He knew better than to forbid her to go, so he voiced his concerns and said, "Chloe, how do you know you aren't walking into a trap? And what about protecting the queen?"

"We don't, but I can't turn away from someone who needs help. Plus, who wouldn't want to go to Hawaii?" She giggled.

"I don't. Once Sabre gets here, we need to find McPherson. So much for us moving closer to your coven and family. I'm sorry, Chloe, and I know how much that meant to you."

"Marcus, I don't care about that anymore. I want to help people, but I want our daughter home and you. I do not consent to you giving yourself to the Tall Dark Man."

"Chloe – not now. Sabre's here. We got to go. Listen carefully to my part of the clue. Find the stone and protect the queen. I will bring our daughter back after we save Malakai and get reinforcements. Stay safe, my love. Now listen to the clue," he said and followed up with the details of his part of the clue. Now, she and Amber could find the stone and keep it safe.

Turning his attention back to the door, he saw the seven-foot Viking standing before him. Sabre sat down and ordered food before he said, "Good to see you again, brother. Never a dull moment, huh?"

Marcus nodded, anxious to get somewhere dark.

"Sabre, can you get the food to go? It's nearly sunrise, and you know what that means."

"Shit, forgot about that, brother. I'll get it to go. Get in the back of my car, and we'll get going. It's going to be a long ride. Don't be surprised to ride in a hearse. It's the only one we have that we use to help transport vampires. The back is sealed with blackout curtains and more. All will be will, my brother."

Sabre called over the server once more and changed the order to go. Marcus left a considerable tip before heading out the door. He turned up his collar to his jacket and thought about Chloe. His wife only wanted her family back, and he owed that to her. Deep down, he hoped that Sabre could drive fast enough to reach McPherson. Before climbing into the hearse, Marcus looked in the back. He noticed Sabre came prepared with a coffin. And of course, the curtains covered every window but the driver's side and the front. Marcus climbed into the coffin and watched as Sabre closed it. He could hear the sounds of the engine starting before he settled in for sleep.

***

Kawika Kekahuna, Honolulu, Present Day

Kawika received confirmation that the package had arrived with the queen. He had hoped she understood the message and would arrive in a month. While waiting at his grandfather's home, he decided to ask his grandfather about his family.

"Exactly what are we, grandfather? An employee told me that her tūtū told her to aid our family whenever asked. We all help one another, but she was pretty adamant when she told me."

His grandfather smiled.

"That pretty girl, eh? She is a beautiful wahine, and I know her tūtū. They are the kupua, and we are the kahunas. Kupuas are destined to help the kahunas in the ways of the goddess Pahulu to protect the island's people. Those that are descended from Pahulu are said to have more mana than any other spiritual advisor. Pahulu was long before Pele. Let her help you, Kawika, and honor our ways. Did you find the queen? The one that we need?"

"Yes, grandfather. I will honor the o'hana and our ways. We will stop the demons from rising. Evil will not come to our islands, and the gods must favor their people and protect us."

His grandfather started coughing, and he knew it was a matter of time before his time would come to meet Kāne. Kawika prepared the potion the doctor showed him to ease his grandfather's pain. As modern as his family tried to be, Kawika was the one who honored the ancient ways and his grandfather. Sometimes, he wished that he could live on the other island, resorting back to the ways of ancient Hawaii.

His grandfather drank the potion and said, "When da queen comes, do what the spirit guides tell you. I have visions that this island will be nothing more if evil wins. When I see the great Kāne, my power will flow into you. You must embrace it more than evah, Kawika. Your father turned his back on the ancient ways because he was scared. But he came back. The whole o'hana will help you. We stand as one and are the strongest kahunas on the island."

Kawika was always a student of learning despite his age. "Grandfather, the kaimoni are coming. Are you sure this queen can defeat them?"

His grandfather coughed once more. "Yeah, grandson. She is the only one who can. The kaimoni, the night marchers, and all the demons in the islands are afraid of those that serve the light and Kāne and da other gods.

Stay true, grandson, to our ways to help the queen."

Kawika promised he would and tucked his grandfather in before leaving. He made sure to say the family prayer for his soul as the time remaining was precious.

On his way home, Kawika had a vision. The kaimoni were walking amongst the locals. He saw Malia standing alone on a rock at Kailua Beach. She was casting her spells, but another kupua was beside her, and she was not a native. This kupua was bathed in silver light, and the two of them were surrounded by the kaimoni. Then he saw what he feared most. A kaimoni attacked Malia and mauled her. He closed his eyes to forget the vision. When he opened them again, the vision was gone.

Chapter Fourteen
Spellbound

Nimue, The Dark Forest, Present Day

Nimue lay on the ground, weakened from the incident with everything. Her eyes opened, and she saw McPherson standing above her, still weak. She labored in her breathing, but the feeling of defeat encompassed her, causing her not to be able to stand. Hours seemed to pass, but McPherson eventually laid down on the earth and slept. The tiger remained vigilant, protecting them.

She must've fallen asleep because gentle hands woke her, startling her. Then she recognized the voice.

"Nimue, Nimue. Wake up. Sabre and I are here. What happened?"

Nimue tried to sit up, but her head was still fuzzy.

"Marcus! You came. Chloe sent a protection tiger. Did you see it?"

Marcus looked around before turning back towards her.

"No."

Nimue rubbed her eyes and searched around for the tiger. She thought maybe the tiger had disappeared when help arrived. Maybe that's what Chloe meant?

"Marcus, we need you to carry the Totem of Death. McPherson tried to, but it was draining him. We need to find the Totem of Life, but there's something you should know."

Before she could tell him another word, she lost control of her body and voice. Through her, the Tall Dark Man said, "Hear me, vampire. I see everything. I am everywhere. This little witch traded her soul for power, and I own her soul. You still need one more totem. Come on, little witch. I will find out what you're up to sooner or later. Come back to me."

Marcus held onto her arms, trying to return Nimue from her trance. Nimue couldn't move, couldn't speak her own words. Her eyes rolled to the back of her head, leaving her in a daze. She could hear the others but couldn't let them know she needed them. She needed Marcus's strength to free her.

"Damn, vampire. Do you think I will let her go that easily, no matter how hard you want to hold onto the little witch? Why not just give in and surrender to me now? You bargained your life for your daughter's so she could learn the dark magic."

Nimue could see Marcus loathing, and she closed her eyes. Letting the power she still had in her control fill her whole being, she said only one word. "*Libertatum.*"

A powerful blast emerged from her, knocking Marcus far away and quieting the voice of the Tall Dark Man inside her head. The light was so intense that Nimue noticed the trees were all burnt around her. Tiny flickers of flames made a path through the trees more profound into the forest.

Nimue reached for McPherson and told him that she was okay. The Tall Dark Man was still with her, but he'd been quieted through her power. She wasn't sure how, but she must be more robust than she thought.

"Marcus! Marcus!"

Turning to the tall man whom she didn't know, she asked who he was.

"Call me Sabre. I am a dire wolf, a member of the queen's inner circle, and I'd like to say, personal friend and bodyguard." He started laughing.

Nimue said, "If we are going to find this totem and help Zaraquel, we must hurry. There's not much time left if the witch Anne is up to something. We need Marcus to carry the totem of death, and no one living can hold it for long."

Sabre said, "Leave that to me. I'll find him."

Before he could head toward the direction that Marcus was thrown, Marcus was already returning to the group. And just in time, Kabos and Rowe appeared out of thin air, and Marcus immediately bowed to Kabos as his way of hugging his old friend.

Nimue found her strength and told them all of the latest events. She held onto McPherson's hand while doing so. The group realized evil had the upper hand this whole time, and this would not be an easy mission. She had heard the stories from Zaraquel about how they could defeat the Tall Dark Man before but this was more terrifying. As she looked at the faces of the others, Nimue realized that they were all afraid, even if they tried so hard not to show it. She wished she could be as brave as they were, even though she was powerful in magic.

Nimue said, "The Tall Dark Man will be with us every step of the way, watching, listening, everything. There's going to be no way to stop him or fool him. I promised I would bring help to save Zaraquel. I do not want to serve him any longer, but I understand if you don't trust me or want me near any of you."

A tear fell from her eye, and she tried to make it stop before she opened the floodgates.

Nimue loved her friendship with Rowe and was sorry for tricking him back in Camelot when he was Merlin. The ghost of Rowe spoke, breaking the silence.

"Nimue, my beloved friend. We all make mistakes in our past lives, present lives, and even future ones. Having you disappear from us is not as simple because evil is afoot. It will make us all train and prepare harder. I think your new friends need you as much as you need them. It's just a matter of you realizing each other's worth. I may not be in a form where I can embrace you to draw out the evil that lurks inside, but all those years of my teaching, do not let the training and time spent teaching you the powers within yourself go to waste. You are a powerful sorceress with more unleashed power than we realized. Trust in yourself and others that evil will not prevail. He will only win if you give up now."

Sabre nodded and embraced Nimue in a tight hold. She felt smothered but welcomed. Marcus nodded and gave McPherson a good old-fashioned slap on the back. Nimue's confidence rose, and she used her power to find the totem of life. Since being welcomed into their family, this was the first time she felt stronger than ever to face the darkness that lay before them.

***

Tituba, Underground, Present Day

Tituba was locked in her room with other witches standing guard. She was no longer permitted to come and go as she saw fit. The master was through with her, and she had other intentions. *Two can play that game.*

Sitting in the middle of a pentagram, Tituba began to chant. Long before she came into his service, she was a powerful witch in Barbados whose power was raw and uncontrollable. Throughout her life, men used her until she discovered her power and strength in witchcraft. Once she learned her inner power, men fell for her, often doing as she bid or succumbing to their secret desires.

"Through time. Through space.
In this life, in the next.
At this hour of the night,
I call upon the power
Bind him to me
I am the queen,
He is the king.
Bring him to his knees."

The underground walls began to shake, and she could hear the witches screaming. Tituba realized that the spell worked no matter where the Tall Dark Man was. Rocks were tumbling down the sides, and pebbles fell to her feet. No one ever paid attention to how powerful Tituba was in her magic. The accusations at the Salem Witch Trials were nothing compared to her true glory.

In Barbados, Tituba learned of the power of sorcery and magic from her mistress. Her mistress convinced her that she would teach her how to protect herself from the devil and his servants.

"Listen to my words, Tituba. You must remember to say it every night from one full moon to the next, and this will ward off evil from you."

Tituba remembered hearing the words and had them memorized by the fourth night. She said them every time she lay on her thin mattress at the end of the long day. Her days flew by; it was a whole month before she knew it. Her mistress was getting sicker but showed her different ways to protect herself. Tituba never thought about what she was learning, but she became an adept student, and all she ever wanted was to protect herself from evil. That was until, one night, she lay in bed, and something woke her up. Her sheets were moving though she lay still. Her heart was beating faster as the sheet was beginning to lift from her body as if someone was underneath. Her hand moved quickly to slap the sheet back down. The thin material fell over her body.

"Who's there? I'm going to scream."

A voice spoke in the darkness.

"Sweet Tituba. Why scream when you called for me all these nights?"

"I did not call for anyone. Who are you?"

The voice laughed. "You asked me to come. Here I am."

Tituba screamed. "Who are you?"

"I am the one you called, and I am the one you seek. You are a witch."

Tituba then realized her mistress was teaching her magic. She felt a lump in her throat and took a long, hard swallow. Somehow she wasn't afraid, but did she hear right? She was now a witch.

"I'm a witch. Aye, I believe I am." Her voice no longer quivered with fear.

"Aye, you are a witch. You invoked the different spells, and you called for me every night. Your mistress was your teacher but needed a successor as her life failed. That is you, my sweet Tituba."

Tituba spoke with a little more confidence. "Then you must be Satan or something. Am I to be your witch?"

The voice laughed. "Aye, you be my witch, but first, you must give yourself to me."

Suddenly the sheet was pulled back, and a man's form appeared over her. Tituba wasn't afraid but could see his handsome face. Her right hand touched his cheek, and her body shook intensely. Her womanhood began to feel warm as if it was hungry for something. She slowly spread her feet apart, waiting. Wanting. As her hand rested against his cheek, he slowly tilted his head and looked into her eyes. Her will was no longer her own. She felt a strong desire to serve him.

She was now his witch and the power grew inside her from that moment on. Tituba swore to herself that she would be his witch until the day she brought him to his knees and made him hers to control.

As Tituba relived that memory, her senses became enhanced as the underground began to crumble around her. Raising her hands to her sides, she flicked her fingers, and the underground stopped collapsing. The door opened, and the witches stopped to stare as she walked through the halls. One by one, magic forced them to kneel to her. Her magic. Her power. It was her time to rise above them all. She was to be the mother to the hunter that the master wanted. She had the power after all these centuries in the underground.

***

Chloe, The Estate, Seattle, Present Day

Chloe and Amber were met at the door by Jerome. He had the most worried look on his face. His clothes were a little disheveled for someone of his position, but Chloe was more concerned about the bruises on his temple and cheek.

"Jerome! What on earth happened-"

She didn't get to finish her sentence before Jerome held up his hand and said, "Miss Tudor, not so loud. My head is quite fragile at the moment. There was an intruder, but I recovered moments before you pulled into the driveway. From what I can tell, everything is still intact and nothing seems missing. However, Miss Stone, the library and your bedroom are untidy. Please excuse me; I fear I need a remedy for this pounding head of mine."

"Nonsense, Jerome! Let's sit in the parlor. I will have you good as new in a few." Chloe helped Jerome to the other room.

After he got settled on the sofa, Chloe stood behind him and placed each hand on one side of his head and said, "Close your eyes. Just relax."

Jerome was quiet. At first, she thought that he might have fallen asleep. But then he shifted his weight some. Chloe chanted:

> "Thoughts, truth, and images
> From your mind to mine
> Show me what I want to see
> Once you show me, I cleanse thee
> No more pain, no more sorrow
> Send to me."

Chloe waited until she saw his shoulders relax so she could close her eyes. She could feel the pain through her fingertips. Then she saw the images, and it made her angry. A dark witch pushed him, then barged into the estate. Chloe could see her face. It couldn't be! The powerful dark witch herself. Raven Hexham. In anger, Chloe gritted her teeth together but knew Jerome's healing must finish. She whispered more chants to remove the bruises and pain from his body. The poor man did not deserve this.

The bruises began to disappear, and Jerome began to move. His right hand felt his cheek and as he turned to face her, Chloe's heart was broken that this man was attacked in one of the group's safest places.

"You are all better now, Jerome. Is there anything I could do for you?"

Jerome patted her hand and said, "No, Miss Tudor. If you and Miss Stone permit me, I would like to retire for the rest of the night, but I assure you, I will rest tomorrow. I am tired from all this activity, but the house will be guarded tomorrow with Kabos' protection spells."

"Of course. Good night."

Once he left, Chloe found Amber trying to clean up the library. Based on the speed with which she put things back into place, she was one pissed off vampire queen.

"Amber, stop for a moment. We need to talk, and it's just you and me right now."

Amber stopped in her tracks, retracted her fangs, and took a few calming breaths. Chloe could see her friend was distraught, but Amber calmed down when Chloe told her about the dark witch breaking in

Amber said, "That fits with the voice I heard. You and I need to find a way to figure out what the fuck is happening here. Malakai is a wolf; Marcus will surrender to the Tall Dark Man for Zaraquel to learn dark magic, and this dark witch breaks in. We need to stop evil in Hawaii. I think it concerns that damn stone and book Michael left me. Could the Tall Dark Man have been planning all this while we reveled in the peace from that battle? I mean, Chloe, it's been three years since the battle."

Chloe paused momentarily before answering because she knew Amber had a strong point. And it was something they hadn't considered. *What if she's right? And this would be how to bring down the queen and all of us?*

Chloe said, "Amber, that certainly is a possibility and a likely one. I mean, all this is happening pretty fast and in three months. We need that stone, and then you and I must figure out what to do while waiting on the others. It's like he's separating us in a calculating way. And we just fell into his trap easily."

Amber grabbed Michael's letter with the directions, and since Marcus gave her his clue's location, they were now prepared to find the stone. Chloe searched the room for anything they could use to cover the stone and keep it hidden as long as possible. Instead she said, "Amber, wait. Let's call the coven. We will need coven magic to keep the stone away from him, and I have an idea."

Amber screamed at her, "I'm tired of waiting. If a dark witch can come in here and hurt Jerome, you and I alone have no chance. I'm going to get that stone. Either give me your clue or come with me."

Chloe needed to reason with her. Amber was in a rage, not just any rage. A vampiric rage. She wasn't going to listen. Chloe had to use her magic on her. Somehow. Her mind began to work overtime and naturally gave in to her power. That's the one thing that made her one of the strongest witches in the world. For her, magic was natural. She closed her eyes and wished to convince her best friend to slow down and think things through. They were up against the Tall Dark Man. When she opened her eyes, Chloe was staring at her best friend through the eyes of a white owl.

"Chloe! Why are you an owl?"

Chloe couldn't speak but landed on Amber's arm. As Amber lifted her arm and once Chloe was directly looking into her eyes, Chloe sent Amber images of things Chloe's vision could only send her.

Amber tried to fight it in her vampiric rage, but Chloe knew that their friendship was stronger than anything put to the test. She kept sending images of a battle, losing Zaraquel, Malakai, and everything her sight sent her. When she was done, Chloe nearly lost her grip on Amber's arm and almost fell but didn't.

Amber caught her and whispered, "You can change back. I understand."

Chloe understood and shifted back to her human form. She laughed, "Thank you, Amber. No matter how often I shift, I can't get used to it, and I've always only been a witch."

"We were all changed by the Blood Moon, and we will never be what we once were. Let's figure out our next step, and I'll be more patient. The Tall Dark Man is back and he's worse than ever."

Chloe called her coven and explained everything that had been happening to them. She revealed her plan of securing the stone but delivering the spell that would hide it using coven magic. They agreed to help.

***

Raven, Eastern Washington, Present Day

Hours later, she pulled up to the base of a hiking trail. She had already woken Arioch and told the demon to prepare for his adventure. The raven that she sent out earlier took them to this location. Raven glanced around and didn't see anything out of the ordinary. They may need to go for a hike, something that didn't appeal to her.

They got out of the car, and Arioch was uncontrollable. With two strong fists, he slammed the ground, causing a massive tremble. Raven lost her balance and fell backward.

"Arioch, I command you to stop. We must sneak in and grab the wolf, and he must remain alive for the master."

Arioch grunted at her as if he didn't listen.

Raven shot a fireball at him and commanded him in a voice that shook the forest. He stopped and fell back in line. Raven motioned for him to follow her as she made her way on a trail. Then she stopped, and she smelled the air.

"Arioch, find the wolf. He's here with others. Kill them all if you must but bring the wolf to me alive. Do as commanded."

Arioch took off, and as she walked, she summoned the master and said, "Master, I found the wolf—the queen's consort. Arioch is going to capture him. I have modified the witch's Book of Shadows. Your plan is coming together. I honor and serve you. We will return with the wolf."

The master spoke to her. "Well done, Raven. You have pleased me with your loyalty. Bring me the wolf soon."

When she caught up to Arioch, he watched the wolves and humans. He hadn't attacked yet but watched closely. She kneeled next to him and watched to see if there were signs of the wolf. She scanned the area, and she spotted the wolf Malakai. He was lying near some others, being well-guarded and sleeping.

She pointed and said, "Look over there. Do you see him?"

Arioch nodded. "Me get the wolf."

Raven realized his communication skills were limited since the spell to enforce obedience was placed on him. She nodded.

"I will clear the way. Kill the others if they get in your way, but try just to grab him and bring him to the car. Less killing the better because it's only the two of us here against all these dogs."

Arioch understood. She watched him go towards the wolf, only to find his path blocked by several wolves. None looked to be the alpha, just lower-level dogs in her eyes. Raven watched Arioch from the distance, keeping out of sight. With one of his arms, she witnessed their decapitations before he continued his path. Raven felt a raw sense of emotion at their deaths because this was the first time she saw his savage strength. Raven began to smile. She was proud of her creation.

Another wolf jumped in the air to attack him from a higher point, but before he could land on Arioch, the demon raised both his arms to catch it. As his hands caught him, Raven realized that Arioch grew in size. She didn't recall her spell giving him that ability. The wolf sat cradled in his arms like hands holding a small marble. Then she saw the two hands clap together, smashing the wolf into broken bits of flesh covered in blood. Blood began to trickle down his stone body, dripping onto the ground.

The other wolves began to appear in clusters of different groups to surround Arioch. Raven used her magic to keep the others motionless. She placed a freezing spell on the ones she could see. The wolves could not move, but they began to howl. Up until now, they appeared to be trying the stealth approach. Raven was getting pissed at their insolence. She decided to come out of hiding and released a circle of fire around each cluster of wolves. Arioch turned to see Raven, so he didn't see the black wolf that appeared out of nowhere approach him.

"Arioch! The wolf! Turn around!"

Arioch turned around and screamed. He threw a fist against one wolf, sending him to the ground on his back. The wolf didn't rise again.

Raven walked through the encampment, unafraid, looking at the wolves' bodies that lay motionless from Arioch's strength. Knowing that Arioch's destruction came from her power, it brought a smile to her face once more. If she ever doubted her magic power before, this proved to her that she was the strongest witch that served the master. She then raised her hand and extinguished the fire surrounding the different wolf clusters. She turned to face the women and children.

"Look at me, dogs. I am Raven. Mistress Witch to the Tall Dark Man. We came only for the wolf – the queen's consort. Get in the way and I will kill you. Swear your loyalty to the Tall Dark Man, not the queen, and you will prosper. Send your big wolf to Seattle at the next full moon with your answer. I will be watching."

Raven released the freezing spell. Arioch grabbed the wolf Malakai, hoisted him over his shoulders and, muttered, "Wolf alive."

The women and children ran, and the black wolf that lay on the ground, rose and charged after Arioch. Raven couldn't let anything happen to either Arioch or the wolf in his arms. Arioch would not be prepared for an attack even though she was sure Arioch would win.

Raven quickly chanted, "*Prohibere*."

The black wolf stopped in his tracks and shifted into his human form. He said, "What have you done to my people? I am Black Wind. You can't take Malakai."

"I am the Dark Witch, and I can do what is needed to serve the Tall Dark Man. As I told the others, come at the next full moon, swear your fealty to him and your pack will reign victoriously. All you need to do is sever the ties with the queen."

"I am Black Wind. The only one who can give that command is the true alpha of this pack. Find him and ask him for his answer."

"Who is the true alpha?"

Black Wind remained silent, infuriating Raven.

"Arioch, beat it out of him. Put the queen's consort down first."

Before Arioch could attack, Black Wind had called for two more wolves to pounce. Instead, Raven and Arioch were surrounded by the whole pack of dire wolves with Black Wind standing in the center. He was clearly the acting leader, so he must be second in command to the alpha. She needed the alpha to force the pack to her master's will. Raven thought if they swore fealty to the master, it would make controlling Malakai in wolf form so much easier, so she said, "We will leave but we are taking Malakai as a sign that we will not play games with your kind. By the next full moon, send your true alpha. He either swears your pack's fealty to the Tall Dark Man or I will return with this demon and your entire pack – man, woman, and child – will die the most painful deaths you can imagine. Do you need Arioch to give an example of my intent? "

Wolves and those in their human form began to show signs of fear and turned to Black Wind for guidance.

"I will give the true alpha your message, dark witch. Now leave our lands. Know that we will get Malakai back, whatever the cost. LEAVE NOW!"

Before they left with Malakai in Arioch's arms, Raven turned around once more and sent fire towards one of their homes. She watched it go up in flames and noticed that Black Wind looked defeated.

Chapter Fifteen
Separated

Kawika Kekahuna, Honolulu, Present Day

Kawika put the phone down and called Malia to his office. He appreciated hearing from Ms. Stone, who agreed to help him, but the tickets needed modification. Ms. Stone requested extra baggage due to the items they needed to bring. Kawika agreed.

Malia appeared, and he began to share with her that Ms. Stone and Ms. Tudor would arrive sooner than planned.

"I need you to make certain arrangements for our guests," he said, "given their unique needs. Make reservations at one of our preferred hotels."

"Yes, Kawika. What about the weird stuff going on in Honolulu? I've noticed it and I know you have too. There's kaimoni around the locals."

He rested his head in his hands, troubled he didn't know what to do. His family, his friends, his island, his people. Kawika finally embraced his family nature and wanted to expand his knowledge of the ancient ways with his grandfather, but time prevented that. Malia put her arms around him and comforted him.

"Malia, Ms. Stone is the queen of all. She has the power to stop them. Begin the preparations because they are coming in two nights' time. The plane comes from Seattle. When the rest of her entourage can come, they will also need special accommodations. I am going to need your help more than ever. Above the internship. Are you willing to help me?"

Malia didn't hesitate when she answered. Kawika was grateful until his secretary brought a man to his office.

"Mr. Kekahuna," she said, "this gentleman doesn't have an appointment but insists on seeing you. I couldn't stop him. He was rather persuasive."

His assistant raised her hands and showed a strange bracelet around her wrists. Kawika noticed that she looked frightened but remained calm the entire time.

He had to give her credit for not making the situation worse. *Who was this stranger?*

The man entered the room. He didn't speak but raised his hand, and a chair moved towards him from one side of the room.

Calmly, he said, "You are what they call a kahuna, are you not?"

Kawika looked at the man. His hat covered most of his face, but his eyes were dark and slanted. His coat was dark and tattered. He had a scar on his cheek and a strange birthmark on his wrist that glowed and caught Kawika's attention.

"Who are you?" Kawika said.

The man didn't say anything at first. Instead, he took a seat, and with a wave of his finger, the assistant's magical bracelets disappeared. Kawika noticed the fear on her face, and he was worried about her.

The stranger smiled and said, "I see you're worried about your assistant. I will let her go. Watch."

The man didn't speak, but Kawika's assistant nodded toward the man and left his office, closing the door. Malia moved closer to him. Kawika's hand tried to reach under his desk for the security button to call the guards, but he couldn't control his arm. His hand was forced on the desk.

The man said, "You won't need security. This is a simple conversation. Call it a history lesson if you need to. Are you ready to listen?"

Kawika nodded since he could do nothing else. He saw that Malia took a seat too.

"You can call me Philip. My family history will sound strange, but you will understand it once you hear the story. The mark on my wrist identifies my ancestors and me with the prophecy. I bear the mark of the serpent. Evil visited my father many years ago to create a line of warriors, strategists, and political men to win over the world, while a line of daughters followed in the darkest of magic. All bear this mark—the mark of the serpent. I am one of those sons. However, my father had a change of heart about this agreement. On the day he was assassinated, he pulled me aside and spoke of a way to break our family curse. A charm was made for me to give to the first daughter, who passed it on to her daughter and so on until a witch with the power of dark magic rose. When light shines in that dark witch, light and dark will clash with an eclipse like no other, and appears in the sky. That has not come to pass, but I sense the stars aligning, so time is near. The dark witch is beginning to question her purpose even though she may not be aware. Now would be a good time for you to ask some questions."

Kawika couldn't believe what he had heard and said, "I am not sure what to ask. This sounds like a book."

"My father was Philip II of Macedon. I'm sure you studied him in history. If I can find the charm and place it on the neck of the dark witch, I can fulfill my father's wish. I carry dark magic in my blood, but I also carry light magic. I am the balance of magic in my family line, but I dreamt there would be another. I must teach the bearer of dark and light magic how to keep the balance before it kills them. I must also protect my family line from being completely sworn to the darkness. My purpose is two-fold, and I have long waited for this day."

Malia fainted and fell against the chair, causing Kawika to stare in disbelief. Between this and the arrival of Ms. Stone in two days, he had his hands full.

He told the new arrival, "Somehow, I believe you. I don't know how I can help you, but someone who might be able to is coming. Can you stay with us for a while?"

Philip smiled. "I am merely here to serve as long as my interests in saving my family are protected. I have lived long and my journey has taken me worldwide in search of the one who will lead me accordingly. Do we have time to talk further?"

Kawika glanced at Malia, who was still unconscious, and nodded. He went to the bar he kept well stocked in his office for the special donors to the museum and started making two drinks.

"Let me make you one of Hawaii's favorite drinks, the Mai Tai, and let's discuss how a kahuna and a kupuna can assist you. I am unfamiliar with the light or dark magic you speak of, but I am in over my head with the kaimoni rising on our island. I have summoned for help from a queen of all the supernatural beings. Her name is Ms. Amber Stone."

Philip took the drink and smiled as if he understood.

"Mr. Kekahuna, apparently, our worlds are not as separate as you may think. I believe — "

"Call me Kawika please. Or David if that is easier for you."

"David, then. Ms. Stone is the queen. She had defeated evil in one of blood prophecy's most epic battles, but evil did not die. This particular evil may be related unknowingly to your troubles here. I have followed the rise of this queen since her destiny came to light in Seattle. Until now, I have tried to find the dark witch that I seek, and I have many eyes in my employment searching for her. One believes that this dark witch is connected to the queen. We are all players in this prophecy – it's just a matter of what side and role you are in this game. Does that make sense?"

Philip finished his drink while Kawika was still comprehending what he had just heard.

Kawika said, "I believe, my new friend, I will have to make more drinks to continue this chat. But first, I see your young friend Malia is coming to."

Kawika approached Malia and offered her a drink.

"Malia, prepare yourself for one of our strangest discussions with Philip. Everything is connected to Ms. Stone and we will need her help more than ever. And I will need your service as kupuna to me."

Malia began to become more alert as Kawika told her what he had just learned. Philip sat back and watched and eventually said, "If I may, David, perhaps I should elaborate more on this story for you and Malia. Where to begin..."

***

Mary, Seattle, Present Day

Mary knew Tabitha's silence would only cause problems for the Tall Dark Man. She decided to report to him. She had watched the other witches summon him before through their connection with him, so she tried it. Mary drew a pentagram, sat on the floor, and said, "Master, hear me, please. It's Mary. Tabitha fell ill due to food poisoning, but we must report in."

She waited.

And waited.

Then, the master answered her call. "Next time, do not wait too long to report in. What is the status of the witch?"

"Master, I will be contacting her today. I wanted to see her habits to find a way to connect with her. Tabitha is watching my baby while I meet the witch. Am I only supposed to friend her or bring her to you?"

"Just friend her. Get her to trust you until I send for you to bring her to me. I have something special planned for the Light Witch Chloe. She will become the final wedge in separating the queen from all her allies and friends."

"Understood, master. Tabitha will report once she is well again."

"You report to me directly. I am losing patience with my plan. Once the witch trusts you, you will bring her to me. The vampire husband has surrendered his life to me; the angel is soon mine, and the witch. The queen's fall from power will be decided. Mary, one more thing. Your baby's life with you depends on you fulfilling this mission. Please me, and I will reward you with your greatest wishes."

Mary released herself from the connection to prevent the Tall Dark Man from learning her true intentions. She went to see Tabitha and found the hag lying in bed, struggling to breathe.

"The master is pleased. He wishes that I continue to report to him as you have fallen ill. His plan continues where I will befriend the witch and earn her trust. Once I succeed, I will restore your power and disappear with my baby. One word to the master, and I will make you regret telling him. Understand me?"

Tabitha meekly nodded and eventually dozed off. Mary watched for a few more minutes to make sure that her spell was working on Tabitha. She looked to be aging and growing weaker by the minute. *All according to my plan!*

Mary decided to wait until tomorrow to reach out to the witch Chloe. She knew Chloe loved her Seattle coffee blends before work, so a casual bump into her might work. Now it was time to play with baby Elijah and make up for her lost time with her son. As she watched him, she realized how much he looked like Valentine. She missed her husband and understood how he died serving the Tall Dark Man, but she didn't blame the queen or any of her friends, even if he died at the queen's hands in battle.

***

Sabre, The Dark Forest, Present Day

Sabre followed behind the others in order to keep watch over them. As the alpha of the dire wolves, it was his responsibility to protect those in his pack as well as those outside the pack. And because the queen awarded him the title Special Protector to the Inner Circle, he felt even more obligated to protect them all. On the way there, Marcus managed to fill him in on everything that had happened since the last battle with the Tall Dark Man. As he understood it, all hell broke loose after three years in less than six months. He gave it a longer time frame than it was because no one knew when the Tall Dark Man had resurfaced. Sabre felt something in the air, but he couldn't put his finger on it since no one needed him until then. He vowed to protect the queen and her friends with his life if need be.

As far as he was concerned, the Tall Dark Man overstepped his authority. He recalled the time when Michael made him swear an oath to protect the queen should anything happen to him. At the time, he never understood what Michael was talking about. That night repeatedly played in his head. It was always the same.

The group was planning for the battle of their lives and Michael was acting strangely. He had just finished hunting with Marcus when he caught Sabre walking the grounds with Black Wind. Sabre knew something was amiss with Michael by his strange behavior, but at the time, he shrugged it off as fear of the upcoming battle like the others had. He knew that some would die and some would survive, but at what cost? The main goal of everyone was to keep the queen alive because should she die, all would be lost. Michael seemed normal when they started talking.

Michael told them, "Sabre, I know Amber has asked you to protect her and the others. But I need you to swear an oath to me. I haven't been myself lately, brother. I think it's the battle and the thought of losing everything I have fought so hard for. If anything happens to me, I need you to protect the queen at all costs. Even if she doesn't ask. I need you to take care of her as if she was your mate, though she isn't. Treat her as such. Will you do that for me, brother?"

Sabre answered, without hesitation, "I swear on my life, my honor and my pack. She will always be protected and taken care of. Should I fall, my second in command, Black Wind, will see to her. I give you my promise. But you will live, Michael. You are one of the chosen vampires."

Days later, Michael was killed by the queen herself. The Tall Dark Man had corrupted Michael's soul, and that was something for which he would never forgive him. Not only did it destroy her, but it also destroyed all of them. Sabre felt that he should've done more to protect them. When the battle ended, he returned to his pack and suffered silently. Sabre maintained contact with the queen but from a distance. He was happy to hear from Marcus and be involved once more, but he hoped he would be the powerful wolf to destroy evil once and for all. He had been waiting for his chance to kill the Tall Dark Man himself and protect his friends, even at the cost of his life. He missed Michael and the friendship they had.

Nimue stopped the group and asked, "Do you feel it?"

No one responded.

Sabre said, "Life is in this section. More life than the other parts and something is here."

Sabre shifted into his wolf form. He sniffed the ground. Then he trotted to Nimue and tugged on her hand. Using a gentle nibble, he guided her to a tree before shifting back.

She said, "It's here. McPherson, can you help me dig? I have to call it from the earth. Once you hold the totem, you will feel stronger, which will be the totem aiding you. You and Marcus cannot be far apart, and he will hold the totem of death while you hold the totem of life. They must be close to each other. Isn't that right, Rowe?"

The ethereal spirit of Rowe nodded.

Sabre shifted back to his human form. He volunteered to do the digging. The last thing he wanted was harm to come to the group. He assumed the role of a strong protector. Reaching the ground, he lifted massive amounts of dirt until his fingers touched something hard. Sabre dug deeper until he could close his hand around an object. As his fingers closed around it, he could feel that it was not large, but not small either. It wasn't a rock, but as he held onto the object, the dirt around his hand felt different. It gave him a strange sensation. He closed his hand around the object and pulled it from the earth. Dirt fell from the totem, and he held it up for them to see. As the dirt loosened and fell from the totem, Sabre looked at it. He could see what looked to be an eagle's head attached to a wolf's body. Wings were spread wide from the top and there were many colors from the eagle's head to the wolf. The wings had blue, red, and black colored feathers while the wolf's body was brown with a light blue. The totem looked ancient. As he held the totem high, Sabre made sure to turn it over and around so that everyone could see this beauty. As he held it, the totem began getting hot in his hands. His fingers were beginning to burn, but it wasn't bad yet because he was strong enough to withstand the heat that was coming from the totem. *But for how long?*

"Nimue, I think this is what you seek. I can feel its power, but it's burning me at the same time. It's getting hotter the longer I hold it."

McPherson stepped forward and said, "Give it to me."

As Sabre handed him the totem, he could see that his skin was already blistering from the heat. McPherson grabbed it and closed his eyes, saying,

"Marcus, hold the totem of death next to my hand. Just don't touch me with it, please."

Marcus took out the totem and held it up for everyone to see. The totem was about the same size but had the head of a snake attached to the body of bull. The only colors on this totem were red, black, and yellow. The eyes on the snake seemed creepy to Sabre. As he stared at the totem, he began to feel his life force draining so he took a large step backwards, away from the totem.

As Marcus and McPherson held the two totems near each other, a flash of light passed between the two. Sabre could feel the power emitting from them from his position away from the two totems. Nimue said her spell and a bright light connected the two totems before disappearing.

"Totems of Life and Death.
Together you are
Apart never more
Let your power rise
Behold the sorceress that will bind
Hear my call
I call for the spirit of Rae
Till I summon you again
Rest together

Now and always."

Each totem remained quiet but connected in the hands of McPherson and Marcus. The group noticed that the forest became brighter than before, and life appeared in the forest.

The trees began to grow more leaves and turn a brighter green while flowers blossomed and turned the once dark forest into what Sabre thought of as a beautiful garden. From the once eerie darkness, the quiet of the area to something that looked picturesque of a garden with the sounds of animals. Bushes were turning green and Sabre even noticed a tree with apples. From the corner of his eye, he spotted two brown eyes looking at them. Even in human form, he had a keen sense of smell and raised his nose to the air. He smiled.

"Don't be afraid little deer. It's safe."

The deer peered his head out from the bushes and began to walk gingerly towards Sabre. He held out his hand and let the deer smell him, followed by a quick, soft lick from its tongue. Sabre went to one of the trees that grew an apple and pulled it down for the little deer. As he fed the deer, he looked at the others with a smile on his face.

He said, "I guess we can't call it the Dark Forest anymore. The plants are alive, and things look better."

The others began to smile and stare at him in amazement as they watched him with the deer. When the deer ran off, he returned to the others.

Marcus grinned and said, "What's next, Nimue?"

She shook her head and said, "I'm afraid to say because the Tall Dark Man will know. We need to save Zara though, and I'm terrified for her. Anne was an awful witch bitch. That was Zara's nickname for her. McPherson, what are we going to do?"

Sabre listened to this and realized he would need reinforcements to protect the totems and the two friends carrying them. These totems sounded essential, and something the Tall Dark Man would want, but Sabre was more concerned about what Nimue had said about the Tall Dark Man knowing what they were up to. He needed to find a way for them to communicate their plans without him knowing. It was up to him to find a way to communicate. He needed Black Wind, his right-hand wolf. He knew his telepathic skills would come in handy to speak to Black Wind if he could just step away from Nimue. He had a plan!

"Kabos, Rowe. Considering you both are spirits, can you protect McPherson and the others while I return to my pack? I need to return since everything seems good now."

Marcus looked at him, puzzled. Sabre simply stood away from Nimue and mouthed, "Follow my lead. It's a plan."

Marcus responded. "We're good. Go on ahead. We'll see each other soon. Thanks, brother, for your help."

The others appeared confused but didn't interject. Sabre said his goodbyes, and Nimue nodded, then turned away from him to see where they would head next from the forest. Sabre quietly stepped away and snuck up behind her. He used his hunting skills to prevent Nimue from hearing him. Then he grabbed her from behind, placing her in a soft but effective chokehold. As her arms began to flail and she tried to put up a fight, she started to lose that fight. Within a few seconds, she was unconscious. Sabre had no intention to harm her but figured that if she was unconscious, then the Tall Dark Man would be unaware of what they would do next. With her unconscious in his arms, Sabre knew that they could continue on their journey. Carefully, he threw her over his shoulder and motioned for the others to follow him.

Sabre knew that Marcus would fill the others in on the plan. He and Marcus had a deep friendship and could trust each other without question. And the ability to formulate a plan on the spur of the moment. He counted on that. As he carried her to the others, he smiled.

"We can continue now without the fear of the Tall Dark Man knowing our every move. This also allows me to contact Black Wind to check on the pack and make sure we are moving forward with haste!"

***

The Tall Dark Man, The Underground, Present Day

He was alone, and it infuriated him. Luckily, his all-time favorite witch, Elizabeth, saved him from whatever spell Tituba was casting on him, but he still felt a little strange. Raven was off on a mission to bring back the wolf, Anne was busy breaking the angel's will, and Mary was trying to cozy up to the witch. He wasn't concerned about the witch's husband, the vampire, because he had already surrendered, and the Tall Dark Man was willing to be patient at the price he made. But the rest, he was not. And he needed his demons. The coven was still making his demon army, and he knew that would take considerable time. He wanted a massive army that would cover the earth in his name.

The Hawaiian gods hadn't called upon him yet, but he knew he owed them whatever price they would request. He only hoped that by the time they came around, it would be too late, or, if luck was with him, the queen would have fallen and he would have his prophecy fulfilled. The Tall Dark Man decided to study the parchments again regarding this dark prophecy. He proceeded down the hall until one of the witches stopped him and said, "Master, we have about three thousand demons created. You will need to name them to control them. Raven had left specific instructions that we have followed. You cannot control them if you don't name them soon." With that, she bowed to him.

"I will come. Find Elizabeth and bring her to the room as well. I will need her power to do that. Your coven has pleased me with the amount you created but I need more. Much more."

The witch smiled at him. "Yes, master."

He learned that only a select few of his witches knew his real name. Knowing his real name would give them power over him, which he now regretted with Tituba based on her damned actions recently. But he still needed her to bear his hunter. A hunter unlike any other. When that hunter rises, none of the races would have a chance.

He entered the room and saw rows of demons just waiting. They all looked like Arioch but with one significant difference. They were not as big as him, which made him wonder why.

"You there. Come here," he said, pointing to a nearby witch.

The witch was a little apprehensive.

"You called, master?"

"They are smaller than Arioch. Why? I need them strong."

The witch began to tremble. She didn't look like she would be able to answer him, but he managed to say, "Raven has been gone so long, and she's the most powerful one of us. Our magic isn't as strong as hers, but we need more stones. I'm sorry, master, if that upsets you."

"What's your name, witch?"

The witch tried her best not to tremble, but he saw her fear. He didn't soften his expression.

"Your name?"

She said, "I am called Margaret. Margaret Bane. You asked for my service while I was awaiting the Great Scottish Witch Hunt of 1597. I am a lesser witch than the others, master, but it is I who serves as midwife to Tituba and Anne, when they bear your children."

The Tall Dark Man recalled that day he summoned her to his service though he paid no attention to her name over the centuries she served him. Her role was clear.

The Tall Dark Man changed the conversation. "Where is Elizabeth?"

"I will search for her and tell her you have summoned for her."

"Go. Find my Elizabeth."

Witch Margaret left to find Elizabeth. While he waited, the Tall Dark Man stared at his army and smiled at the thought of his demon army walking the earth, swallowing up its inhabitants, leaving a wasteland just waiting for his other monsters to rise. He began to smile until he saw Elizabeth from the corner of his eye.

Witch Elizabeth approached him. "Here I am. How may I serve?"

Ah, my Elizabeth. The most powerful Hexham witch of them all. Sometimes he wondered if she should be the one to go after the wolf so Raven could lead the coven in making demons.

"My Elizabeth. Provide the coven with more magical stones. Tell me if I should have you bring me the queen's wolf instead of Raven. She's taking far too long to bring me the wolf."

"No, master. I fear Tituba is not done with her spell casting. It will take both of us to watch over her to deliver the hunter."

He thought for a moment and realized she was right. *He needed Tituba to pay for her insolent behavior against him!*

"Make it so. I need to be alone. Provide the stones and then keep Tituba away from me. Chain her up if you have to. Just don't let her near me."

He found himself alone once more, but this time surrounded by parchments of the ancient ways. The Tall Dark Man wanted to know more about this dark prophecy that would bring the angel to him, the world to kneel before him, and the rampage of the demons. He shuffled through the various parchments and found another part of the prophecy.

Two by birth
One of light, one of dark
Marked by a prophecy that on the
darkest night
At the witches' hour
Magic will die when the two meet face
to face

The sun and the moon will collide
Until a battle fulfills the ancient
prophecy.....

Until what? The parchment was ripped. He wondered if this was another parchment damaged during one of those tumultuous times between him and the True One. Who was this girl? In his entire lifetime, he figured he was the boy but who was the girl? It's not the angel, not the queen. Crumpling the paper, he was so upset that he didn't care and threw it against the wall. The only thing that made sense was that the dark prophecy was in his favor. For once, he would be victorious. All the actions that he had taken so far had made him victorious over the queen. It was just a matter of time before she fell.

He summoned Anne. He wanted updates on the angel. The angel was all he could think about lately. His angel. Maybe it was time to bring her to him. She would be guarded and separated from her family and the queen. The angel would be his and only his. Separated. The thought appealed to him, but he called upon Loquiel, once in his service, but dismissed upon his failure in his mission to report on the angel. Loquiel was the only one who knew the inner secrets of the angel. He hoped Loquiel would provide helpful information. The Tall Dark Man wondered if he would serve him again, knowing the angel was to be his bride. Loquiel appeared before him and bowed. As a fallen angel, he had the power to appear and disappear as needed.

"You summoned me? Why?"

"Loquiel, I have need of you once more if you are willing to enter my service again."

Loquiel didn't say anything, which made the Tall Dark Man angrier.

"Answer me, Loquiel."

"What do you require of me, master?"

The Tall Dark Man studied the fallen angel before him.

"The angel that you fell in love with, the one I ordered you to help conduct an unjustified kill. Do you remember?"

"Yes, master."

"According to the dark prophecy, one that has been proving useful to me, I can finally have my revenge against the queen if the angel becomes my bride. She is learning the dark magic now from Witch Anne. I want you to work with Witch Anne to use the angel's desires and secrets against her. To make her mine."

Loquiel didn't answer but shifted in his stance, looking uncomfortable. He watched Loquiel's mood momentarily before breaking the awkward silence.

"You can serve me again and reap the rewards of my power to destroy the queen or I will banish you once more."

Loquiel nodded. "I will serve, master. I will go to Witch Anne and help with the angel. She will be yours."

Chapter Sixteen
Hawaiian Welcome

Chloe, The Estate, Present Day

Amber was drained magically from trying to use her power as the queen to locate Zaraquel. Ever since her birth, Amber and Zaraquel had a strong bond that was part of the prophecy. Amber promised to try to find where Chloe's daughter was before they left Seattle. Hunting was even a task for her when Chloe finally convinced her to give her the clue, and since she knew Marcus' clue, she could search the ground for the stone. It didn't take much for Amber to agree, but it did take Chloe several hours to get Amber to return to her coffin to rest. This was the one part that Chloe loved the most. She had the estate practically to herself during the day.

This allowed her and Jerome to work together on warding the estate with magic and for her to learn more about Kabos' history.

Before she dug up the stone, Chloe wanted to visit the museum and get her coffee. She knew she needed to arrange for the exhibits to be returned if they left Seattle. Part of the arrangement Amber made with Kawika was that Chloe would escort the exhibit back to Hawaii to ensure the collection would not be compromised. This way, no one would question why she and Amber would be gone at the same time Malakai supposedly took a leave of absence. It was part of the plan.

Chloe entered her favorite coffee shop. The smell just made her feel relaxed. It was always her favorite place in the morning. As she awaited her order, she noticed a young woman eyeing her. Chloe was cautious but smiled back until the woman approached her and said, "You must be Ms. Tudor. My name is Mary and I wanted to congratulate you on that fabulous exhibit of Hawaiian artifacts at the museum. I was most impressed with this collection."

Chloe relaxed and extended her hand for a handshake, saying, "Thank you. I wanted to capture the soul of Hawaii through this exhibit. It's always nice to hear such praise and admiration from our visitors."

As Mary shook her hand, Chloe suddenly got a faint vision. It wasn't as strong as her regular visions but was enough to frighten her a little. Her vision showed this woman and a man that looked exactly like Valentine. It couldn't be.

"My name is Mary. I had studied art many years ago, but I was going to stop by the museum to see about any job opportunities you might have."

Chloe needed to think. And fast. She quickly said, "I could use an assistant. I talked to my supervisor about it the other day, but nothing is official. What if you left your contact information with me, and I can call you when I'm ready?"

Mary was quiet but finally said, "Could we visit your office? I'd like to know what I'm getting into before considering anything. And I'm new to Seattle that I don't know my way around."

"Sure, let's go there now. You can tell me all about you on the way."

Chloe listened as Mary told her about her life. She was married young and loved her husband more than anything, but he was brutally murdered in front of her and their young baby. As she listened, Chloe kept one hand hidden where she could weave a spell to try to see into her story. Something kept her blocked. The story was an interesting one, but she wondered if it was true or not.

"Chloe, mind if I ask you a hypothetical question?"

"Go ahead."

"If you hire me as your assistant, would I be able to learn from you too? I hear you have amazing gifts for recognizing artifacts and learning about their origins. I would love to learn from you."

Based on everything that had happened, Chloe became uneasy with that question, but she had to keep up appearances for her role at the museum.

"Of course," Chloe said, "Just know that I'm not really a teacher, so I don't mean to be rude if I come across that way."

Mary laughed. "I think we will get along fine."

Chloe remained silent on the way to the museum. As they entered the museum, Chloe showed Mary the reception area where visitors enter and pointed to a hallway that led to several offices for the staff. She led the way down that hallway towards her office when Malakai's assistant appeared and handed her a fax that arrived from Kawika Kekahuna. She looked at it.

Ms. Tudor:

It would honor the state of Hawaii
if you would accompany our artifacts
back to their rightful home. A ticket is
waiting for you at the counter of
Hawaiian Air at the Seattle
International Airport. All other
arrangements for your stay in Hawaii
have been made.

Mahalo,
Kawika Kekahuna

"Grace, we must prepare today's exhibit to return home to its people. I will also accompany the artifacts, but Malakai and I discussed needing an assistant to help me with my exhibitions and research. Mary might be a good fit, but I won't be here to train her. Any thoughts on who can assist with Malakai on leave and a scarce crew with people's vacations?"

Chloe knew Grace was keen on some of their unusual activities and could keep an eye on Mary because Grace was part of Malakai's pack.

Grace nodded but gave Mary an unusual look as Grace said, "Mary, we will need you to fill out paperwork. You can do that here while I talk to Ms. Tudor about her travel."

Grace provided the paperwork and showed Mary where she could complete it. Chloe brought Grace to her office but not before asking security to monitor the applicant. They had a great friendship, and she knew she could trust Grace with anything. In fact, if anything happened to Amber or Malakai, Chloe and Marcus had asked Grace to look after Zaraquel should they die.

When the doors closed, Chloe said, "I can't read Mary. Something is keeping my magic blocked, but I can see some things. I don't like it. Too much is happening right now, all at the same time. We are divided. I know it's because of the Tall Dark Man but I can't figure out the why and the how."

Grace put her hand on Chloe, and she felt a tad better.

Chloe looked at Grace and said, "What are you?"

"I am not just a wolf. I, too, am a witch, but not as strong as you. Malakai prepared our pack since that dark witch came in here. Leave Mary to me. I might be able to get somewhere with her, but you should know something. I see people's auras. Hers is black but not entirely black. It's changing somehow. Malakai left specific instructions to aid you and Amber with whatever you need to save him, but you are first to save all of us if you can before him. He was strict about that, knowing the queen would have a different heart, considering he's her consort. He was willing to sacrifice himself for all of us. You need to be sure to follow that."

Chloe nodded and said, "Find out what you can about Mary and keep me posted. We're going to Hawaii. Too bad Marcus isn't with me. Perfect romantic place, but he's off in the woods with McPherson and Sabre."

Chloe left Mary in Grace's care and headed to the exhibit room to help package the items they needed. It would be a long day before they started to head overseas.

****

Anne, The Witch's Cottage

Anne dawdled after the Tall Dark Man left, watching the angel sleep. As she placed her two fingers on Zaraquel's forehead, she whispered a spell that would speed up the darkness inside Zaraquel before waking her up. Anne noticed the red in the wings that would not darken and began to wonder how mighty this angel was. Before she could turn her back to allow Zaraquel to wake, she noticed that the angel was changing.

A bright light encompassed her body, and her facial features changed. Zaraquel was aging by just a few more years. Anne knew she was already eighteen per their conversations, but now, her student looked like she was in her mid-twenties. *Incredible!* She was intrigued. Anne reached her hand to touch the light that covered the angel, but, as soon as her fingertip touched the light, she was thrown back against the wall. Scared to watch what would further happen, Anne left the room shaken. The last thing she needed was to fail her master with the angel. The angel was her most important task in all the years of serving him, including birthing his demons.

She knew that Zaraquel came here with a backpack. She went to her room to see what she had kept in there. Opening the backpack, she found a notebook, a journal, a picture of her family, and a few trinkets. Nothing useful but the journal. Anne decided to read it. She thumbed through the pages to just read a few entries.

> Sometimes my mom doesn't get me. I
> lost Rae. That hurt me the most. She
> doesn't understand that I am different
> from all my friends. Auntie Amber
> doesn't get it either. I have to find a way

to bring Rae back. I'm just so lucky I found Nimue. She gets me. But she's still not Rae. I need Rae.

It's been a minute since I wrote in here. Dad allows me to be me. He's the coolest dad even if he's a vamp and can practically eat the parents of all the bullies in the world. Uncle Michael was the best but he had to die. I wonder what it would be like if dad would let me become a vampire.

So the witch bitch is supposed to be teaching us dark magic. Nimue doesn't like her. I think she's kinda cool but she's weird. I hope she teaches me what I need to bring Rae back. I need to get outta here soon. The witch bitch doesn't cook well but I hear my mom's voice, "Mind your manners." And all that blah blah stuff she nags about. I wonder what came of Loquiel. I loved him first but he lied to me. What if he could change?

Anne wondered if she could use this to her advantage. Zaraquel wanted something, but what would she be willing to give up in return? She heard a rumble in the closet, and something crashed.

"Who's there?" Anne yelled. "Who's in my cottage?"

Anne quietly moved towards the closet to open the door, but whatever was there vanished. Anne used her magic to cast a dark spell on the room, dimming any light magic the angel would try to use. Then, she went through her cottage using the same spell to prevent light magic from being cast. She returned to the room where she kept Zaraquel to find her waking up.

Anne said, "Angel, how do you feel? Are you strong enough to learn more dark magic? We should try to finish your learning so that you can return home. Wouldn't you like that, dearie?"

Zaraquel looked at her strangely and mumbled, "What happened?"

Anne smiled and said, "You needed to rest to let your body learn to balance light and dark magic. We can't let one rule over the other, right?"

Zaraquel nodded but didn't say anything further. Anne took this moment to hand her a mirror. She watched as Zaraquel studied herself in the mirror. The angel didn't seem affected by her change. Anne wondered why.

"Angel, you aged. It's like you grew up some. Why is that?"

Zaraquel answered matter of factly. "I'm the daughter of a witch and vampire. I belong to one of the highest orders of Avenging Angels. I'm rather tired, Anne. I'm not sure what else is wrong, but I feel strange. Can our lessons wait?"

"Yes, dearie. They can wait. Go and lay down in your room."

***

Ku, Hawaiian God, Present Day

Ku surveyed the islands, and he was hungry for a sacrifice. So much had changed on the islands over time. The ancient ways were becoming lost except to a few. He lost his idol but something inside him kept him connected to it. He could feel it but couldn't see it. This idol meant a lot to him. He was a god but couldn't find the one idol he made for a wahine so long ago. That deserved a war all on its own.

He was also missing his mace. His powerful weapon held the souls of those that were sacrificed to him. He couldn't even remember when he lost it, but it might have been during one of King Kamehameha's battles in which he helped him to unite the islands. The king thought he was uniting the land and the people under one ruler, but Ku had other intentions. He wanted the largest island to swallow the lesser islands to assert his dominance over Kāne but failed.

He needed his mace to aid the kaimoni, set free on the islands once more. The locals could not see the kaimoni in their demon form, making Ku eager for his war. In fact, the kaimoni looked like the other islanders, so they blended in real easy in order to attack their prey. He recalled the stranger that came to visit some years ago. The stranger owed him a debt he intended to collect, but knowing his brother, someone would be brought to the islands to stop him. Ku decided to wait, but he would call upon the stranger soon. It was just a matter of time.

***

McPherson, The Dark Forest, Present Day

Sabre carried Nimue and led the way, followed by Marcus, Kabos, and Rowe. McPherson brought up the rear. The two totems had to be in proximity to each other, and they could maintain that connection since Kabos and Rowe were spirits. McPherson didn't feel right calling Rowe, once known as Merlin, a ghost.

As they walked, McPherson said, "We need to get to the Order. I need to find the spell Zaraquel would use to bring Rae back."

Sabre nodded and led the group in that direction. There was an opening at the edge of the forest, and that's when Marcus' phone rang.

He answered it. The others waited while he heard the call from the other end before saying, "Chloe, whoa, settle down, baby. McPherson and I have the totems. We also have Nimue, but there's a problem. The Tall Dark Man can hear and see through her. We need to be careful. Sabre knocked her out but she's safe. What's wrong?"

McPherson watched Marcus' body language for clues, but that's when Marcus put the phone on speaker for all to hear.

Through the tiny speaker, Chloe said, "Amber can't locate Zara. She tried with all the magic she had, but it weakened her. We are to fly to Hawaii to help another witch with his problem. I think it's related to our situation. We're all being separated for a reason, and it's all done by the Tall Dark Man."

McPherson couldn't resist asking, "What do you mean? By 'him.' How in the hell is he that powerful again? I thought we destroyed his armies and all."

Chloe said, "He's back. You know that part, but it's just weird. My sight doesn't lie to me; things don't feel right. So, Marcus, I need you to stay with us longer. Do NOT give yourself to the Tall Dark Man. Promise me that. PROMISE! We need you. I need you."

Marcus spoke quietly. "I promise. Not until Zaraquel is safe with you. I gave my word unless you could find a way to stop him. But I will stay with McPherson. Our totems are linked and no one else can touch the totem of death. I'm sorry, honey. I honestly thought I had no other choice but that one to save Zaraquel and bring Rae back from the dead for her."

McPherson heard that Marcus was a broken man. Kabos whispered something to Rowe that he couldn't hear. Rowe smiled and that gave McPherson hope.

"McPherson, tell Chloe that Marcus will remain with us. Give her hope. I think we have an idea when the time comes but we have to go now," Rowe said.

"Chloe," said McPherson, "we know what to do where Marcus will remain with us. We need to go and learn what Zaraquel was going to do. The spell to bring Rae back from the dead is powerful. It's playing necromancy, a form of dark magic that I dislike using or teaching. I don't like being separated from one another at this time, but you and Amber must go. We must also save Malakai and learn what Zaraquel has to do with the totems. We will be together again real soon. Remember to bring your emergency craft bag that I made for you. If her magic is drained, Amber may be out of commission for a few days. She will need fresh blood when she wakes. Protect her coffin with the spell we created for her and Marcus. It should work only on vampires."

"Got it. We didn't feel safe retrieving the stone. Jerome guards our answers, but to ensure he gives it to you, say 'Flesh, Blood, and Bone'. With his permission, I cast a spell on him to safeguard our answers and to protect him. God Speed, Marcus, and all of you. Bye."

Marcus ended the call, and that's when McPherson noticed the blood tears on Marcus's face. McPherson tried to cheer his friend up, but they had to hurry to the Order.

Chapter Seventeen
Demons Galore

The Tall Dark Man, The Underground, Present Day

He sat on his throne, tapping his long fingers against the armrest. He had heard from Raven that Arioch had captured the queen's consort. The wolf was his! While he waited, he took out one of the parchments from his library. The words fascinated him because it was in a language unknown to him. He could read a few words he recognized because they were names. He knew these names. Kabos. Eshmun'azar. Illyris. And then there were names he did not recognize.

The Tall Dark Man called one of the witches to him and said, "Where is Tituba? She should be nearby so that I can keep an eye on her. She is..." He paused. "With child."

This witch appeared nervous but answered him, "She

is powerful, master. She forced us to submit and no other witch could do that to us but Raven. Maybe Elizabeth… but Raven is the one we listen to.”

“What's your special craft, witch?”

The witch closed her eyes and took a deep breath. “Master, I am able to create illusions that can trap someone physically. Similar to playing mind games with the victim. I am very good at my craft. They call me Brinna.”

He grew angry at not knowing the whereabouts of Tituba but acknowledged Witch Brinna with a nod. He rolled up the parchment and instructed the witch to return it to his library. The Tall Dark Man rose and shouted so that all could hear him.

“Tituba! Come forward to me as I command you. Or feel my wrath against you.”

From the underground walls, Tituba's voice echoed back, “Master, I am with your child, who grows inside me. I will not come to you as you demand. You will come to me by order of your name.”

“*Pueri mei faciens.*
Venator meus.
Veni ad me parere solum me.”

Within minutes, Tituba was in front of him. He stood and raised his hand, forcing her onto her knees. He made sure he did not hurt his hunter. Reaching for her womb, the Tall Dark Man touched her belly. The child responded to him. Then, a witch brought a drink to him.

"Drink this," said the Tall Dark Man. "It will not harm you, but it is needed for the hunter within you. Soon, you will birth the mightiest of hunters, but till then, he needs certain nourishment that only I can provide."

The Tall Dark Man watched, but Tituba did not reach for the goblet. His patience was wearing thin with this witch.

Finally, she broke the silence between them and said, "I command you, Sammael. Not the other way around."

The nearby witches gasped at the use of his real name. Few who served him knew his real name. He felt her control over him. Clenching his fist, he fell under her command though he fought hard against it.

He repeated his spell one more time. The spell that brought her to him. The child, the hunter, obeyed him already. Tituba must've felt his control because she screamed his name louder.

With the power in his right hand, he blasted Tituba away from him. Then, the Tall Dark man heard a voice calling to him.

"Father. Hear me. I am the hunter you chose to create. I will obey. I will free you from this mother's grasp. Watch and learn."

He smiled at the voice of his hunter. Suddenly, next to him, Elizabeth appeared.

"I was summoned, master, but not by you."

The Tall Dark Man looked at his beloved witch. He was no longer in control. Even though he pushed Tituba physically away, her hold on him was strong. He had never lost to a witch in all these centuries. Never. He was furious but needed Tituba's body to nourish the hunter until it was time. His eyes pleaded with his witch Elizabeth, and she nodded.

He watched as Elizabeth strolled over to Tituba. As Elizabeth weaved her arms and chanted a powerful spell, Tituba rose in the air. Tituba tried to resist but Elizabeth weaved her spell more forcefully.

"Foolish bitch," said Elizabeth. "I am the master's witch. My line begins before any of you. Through my line, the most powerful witches serve the master. Therefore, you will serve me in his place. Do you understand?"

Tituba fought Elizabeth while the Tall Dark Man just watched. He hoped that nothing would happen to his hunter, but he trusted Elizabeth with her intent. He watched as Tituba summoned her magic fireballs and aimed them directly at him. Luckily, he saw that Elizabeth had quick reflexes, and with one word, the fireballs shot at the wall. Sparks were flying and the two witches fought against one another. Deep down, he trusted Elizabeth with his life. He knew she would not let anything Tituba could conjure injure him.

The witches around him began to comfort him the best they could and helped protect him from the magic spells flying back and forth. The Tall Dark Man realized that all the witches heard Tituba use his real name. Inside, he was seething with hatred at Tituba even though he still needed her body. Elizabeth was weaving spell after spell to make Tituba powerless enough to release her hold on him and submit to Elizabeth.

The Tall Dark Man realized none of the other witches dared say his name. Tituba was beginning to slow down in her magic because Elizabeth managed to avert every fireball approaching him. Elizabeth was his most powerful witch. The others were watching in awe, not afraid of getting hit, because they had trust and respect in Elizabeth's powers. Out of nowhere, Tituba closed her eyes and summoned a familiar – a black panther. She commanded the panther to scare the other witches as they ran from him – all but one. He began to wonder if Elizabeth would be defeated by this miserable bitch. He was beginning to feel powerless.

His mind raced to the thought of the wolf. *Where is Raven?*

One witch, who brought him the drink earlier whispered in his ear, "Master, we serve only you. But there are some in your inner circle that have been helping Tituba. What can we do?"

There was a way, but he would have to ultimately trust this little witch. He didn't know her well, but what other choice did he have? Using the last of his own free will, he said to her, "My name."

Tituba must have been more powerful than he gave her credit for because before the little witch could make her move, Tituba cast a spell that obliterated the little witch. One minute the witch was standing right next to him and the next, he was covered in her pieces of flesh. *Fuck!* With no other witches around him, he was left vulnerable and with little to no control. The Tall Dark Man didn't even have the power to wipe off as much of the little witch's flesh that covered him.

He heard the hunter's voice once more.

"Give me my name, father. Control me to do your will. Let me be your instrument."

The Tall Dark Man answered through his mind, "Then Tituba will know your name. Your name must be as sacred as mine. Help my witch Elizabeth if you can, my son."

He was losing the last of his free will while Tituba was not under his control. Hanging his head down, he could see his plans slipping away should Tituba fully control him.

Hearing Elizabeth once more, he raised his head. *Could Elizabeth save me?*

She yelled, "TITUBA! I command you. Break your hold on the master now, or I will destroy you, and your power will be mine. Hear me, witch!"

Tituba began to look defeated, but she raised her hand once more.

"You are mine, Sammael. I command thee to serve me."

With that statement, Elizabeth spoke the words of power he gave her all those years ago when he first taught her the spells.

"I am the first of the line to come.
I am the power you seek but do not
have.
I am the fire that controls you.
I will be the fire that binds your
power.
I will be the hate that you bear.

I remove your power, your name.
Till the end of time."

Tituba collapsed to the ground and breathed heavily. Elizabeth almost collapsed but the Tall Dark Man saw that she remained standing but unsteady. Then, he saw his witch return to his side.

"For I am the first of the line to serve
you.
I hold your name and power in my
hands.
I return to you, master, your name.
I return to you, master, your power.
I serve you till the end of days."

The Tall Dark Man regained his power and control. He saw that his witch was weak. He owed his life to his Elizabeth. He invigorated her once more, restoring and increasing her power.

"Bind Tituba," he said, "but keep her body safe. The hunter is well but not ready yet."

The witches slowly came forward, out of hiding, after the magic fight and took care of Tituba.

One witch said, "We will secure her in a room to

watch over her till he is born. We serve you, master."
And she left without another word while the others
carried Tituba to her new room.

***

Raven, The Underground, Present Day

Raven and Arioch finally made it back to the lair
with their prize. The wolf proved to be a handful, but
with a few threats along the way, he was easily
controlled. Arioch dropped the leash, but the wolf didn't
run away. He was smelling the air.

Arioch said, "Master in trouble."

Raven looked at him and used her power to sense what
was wrong.

She said, "Find him. Protect him."

She grabbed the leash and went to the Tall Dark
Man's room. It was the first place she thought to look.
Raven saw Elizabeth standing next to the master,
guarding him. The witches had stopped making the
demons. She didn't get an easy feeling when she asked,
"Matriarch Elizabeth. What happened? Is the master
alright?"

Elizabeth stepped aside and motioned for her to come
forward.

The Tall Dark Man said, "I am fine now, Raven. Elizabeth took care of our little problem. I see you brought me the queen's consort. Is it true that he cannot shift back to human form?"

Raven smiled. "Yes and no, master. First, are you sure you are alright? I sent Arioch to protect you. He should be around here."

Then she saw Arioch searching the room to ensure the master's safety. The last thing Raven wanted was anything happening to the master.

The Tall Dark Man spoke while shifting in his seat. Even though Raven wasn't fully aware of what happened, she could tell the master looked weak.

"Tituba seemed to have gotten the silliest idea that she could control me. But Elizabeth restored my power, but it will take time to regain my strength, and the hunter will obey me. I only need that useless witch alive till she births the hunter. Now, tell me, can Malakai the wolf shift?"

"There is a way but only by invoking the word of power I placed in this curse. Only I know the word. Let me whisper it to you so the wolf doesn't hear. I wouldn't want him to try to figure out how to escape and let the others know."

"Agreed. Come forward."

She looked down at Malakai and said, "Sit, dog. Then we will begin the next part of your new life."

Raven leaned close to the master's ear and whispered, "Say his name backward. Then he will shift on your command."

The Tall Dark Man smiled.

"Well done, Raven. Now, take your dog and finish the demons. The witches need your guidance and power after our little incident today. We don't have enough stones for the army of demons I need under my command. See what you can do."

Elizabeth smiled at the master and then at Raven. Raven knew to respect her family matriarch and bowed in reverence.

***

The Hunter, Underground, Present Day

"Father, father. Can you hear me calling?"

The Tall Dark Man answered his call.

"My son. The hunter. Has Tituba hurt you?"

The hunter realized that his father, his master, was waiting for him to do something important. He listened, hoping something would become clear to his purpose, but his answer was silence. Though he was inside

Tituba's womb, he was all-knowing because his father created him. He had memories of two different lives that he must've lived before. One of such violence and hatred, while the other was something of mystery and purpose.

"Name me father. I can't serve you while inside this host body. I see into her thoughts. Let me serve you now. This witch is not done with you yet."

"My son, my hunter. Tell me, what is my name?"

The hunter giggled. "I do not need your name. I need to exist to do your will. Your army will be my army. I will become the master that you need to bring you to victory. I cannot rise until you will it. The longer the witch keeps me inside, you are in danger, Father. I see and feel all around me."

Again he was met with silence. He listened to the witch's thoughts. She planned to send Father to his demise once her powers were unbound. Patience was not something he was going to like.

"FATHER! Tell me to rise and I will rise. I will undo this witch and you can unleash my fury."

The Tall Dark Man spoke to him once more. "Rise, my son. Rise, my hunter. You will rise with the last potion I need the witch to drink. "

"I will rise. Come to me, Father."

With that said, the hunter made the witch scream in unbearable pain as he began to rise from her womb. The birth was at hand. The rise of the hunter was inevitable.

***

The Kaimoni, Ancient Hawaii

The kaimoni wandered the land after one of Kamehameha's battles, parading around the fallen warriors. Kapuni was one of the fallen warriors but wasn't dead yet. Through the corner of his eye, he watched as they slowly inhabited warrior after warrior. He slowed his breathing as one of the kaimoni stood over his shoulder.

The kaimoni reached his hand down and pulled up Kapuni's head. Faking his death was not easy. The kaimoni rolled his body over, and Kapuni's eyes opened in reaction.

The kaimoni smiled at him.

"Warrior, you are mine."

Before Kapuni could say anything, he found himself inhabited by the kaimoni. He screamed.

Kapuni stood up, grabbed his spear, and looked at the remaining warriors on the ground. It was hard to fight this evil that was now inside him. He walked to another fallen warrior and touched the man's chest. He was still breathing.

"Kaimoni, hear me. I am your leader. Find a warrior still breathing and enter his body. Take him before his soul leaves to return to Kāne."

One by one, the kaimoni entered the fallen warriors, still breathing.

***

Kawika Kekahuna, Honolulu International Airport, Present Day

He had received special clearance from the state and TSA to wait at the arrival gate for his guests and the exhibit's return. The state of Hawaii had no intention of losing its ancient artifacts and placed Kawika on the highest clearance possible for the airport. Through his extraordinary gifts as a kahuna, he could see the many kaimoni that were disguised among the different humans. Since he asked Malia to come with him, he leaned over and whispered, "Do you see the kaimoni too?"

Malia tilted her head, allowing her black hair to fall

loosely to one side.

"Yes. It's like we humans are outnumbered."

"Ms. Tudor will arrive, and we arranged for Ms. Stone's carrier to be with the exhibits. Since it is night here, Ms. Stone will be awake. I ensured her flight would allow her some flexibility while booking their flight as private. Keep an eye on the kaimoni and I will keep watch for the plane."

"You got it. I appreciate you trusting me, Kawika. I mean with your family secret, and I trust you with mine. It's hard to keep da kine secret, you know."

"Malia! Ms. Stone and Ms. Tudor are our guests. They do not know our local pidgin speak. And we must consider them like royalty of our kind. She is the queen of all."

"Proper English. Got it, boss."

Kawika rolled his eyes. Then as Malia walked about the area, watching for the kaimoni, the plane arrived. Since the flight was private, he hoped the wait wouldn't be long. After thirty minutes, the doors opened and a woman with black hair and a strand of white hair emerged, followed by a redhead. Both women were quite exquisite looking, but the red-headed one was excited. Kawika thought that must be the queen because when he spoke to her on the phone, she was excited to hear his request for help. He assumed that only a queen would be that excited.

He waved his hand in hopes that the two women would see him. One did, and they both hustled over to him.

"Hi, I'm Chloe. This is Amber. Are you our contact from the museum?"

"Aloha! I'm Kawika. David is the English translation. All arrangements have been made, courtesy of the Honolulu Museum and the state of Hawaii. Please accept these leis as a warm welcome."

Kawika placed the plumeria leis around their necks with a gentle kiss on the cheek. He noticed that both carried a small bag with them and Chloe's bag was a bit larger than Amber's bag. Chloe must've caught him looking at her bag and smiled at him.

"David, I took the liberty of carrying some of the artifacts on the plane with me. I wanted to feel their history before arriving, so these are probably the most valuable in my opinion and hey gave me a sense of what we are facing."

People were walking around them, ignoring their conversation, but he noticed some strange behaviors of some of the locals. It wasn't overwhelming so he made sure to pay attention to two women in front of him.

Amber said, "Thank you, David. We plan to learn the Hawaiian language while we are here. I feel like I'm a little drunk but that's to be expected. I had to feed while on the flight due to a little magical problem. Is there somewhere we can talk and get up to speed on things before the sun comes up?" Amber asked.

Malia found her way over and didn't bother with introductions. She was too anxious and said, "Kawika, we need to do something. The kaimoni are pulling aside some humans for help, and the humans, well, they disappeared."

Before he could answer, a voice came over the loudspeaker.

"Mr. Kekahuna. Is there a Mr. Kekahuna in the terminal? We request your presence at the desk."

Kawika looked around and asked, "What did you see, Malia?"

"The kaimoni. They are everywhere."

"Hi, I'm Amber. You must be David's intern. What are the kaimoni?"

David said, "Ms. Stone, my apologies. This is Malia. Kaimoni is our word for demons. You are familiar with demons, right?"

Amber giggled. "I'm the queen. Let Chloe and I help you. It's why we came here without our whole team."

She turned to the other woman and said, "Chloe, use

your sight and connect to me. Show me what you see."

Chloe looked around for a moment and said, "You might want to sit for what I will show you. Amber – it's not like anything we've seen in Seattle."

Kawika motioned for them to sit in a quiet section while he went to the counter. As he started to get closer to the counter, Malia came up behind him and pulled him back. She whispered, "Trap. We need to go back to the queen."

Kawika stopped in his tracks and returned with Malia to the women.

Chapter Eighteen
All Hell Breaks Loose

Zaraquel, The Witch's Cottage, Present Day

Zaraquel was still groggy but awake enough to get her bearings. She remembered the witch putting her to sleep to help her body, but she felt different. Finding a mirror, she stared at herself and started running her hands up and down her cheeks. She aged again. Her quick aging process has slowed down for years due to her justified kills, and, according to McPherson, it would slow down long enough for her to enjoy life with her family.

Her family. Rae. Nimue. She was letting them all down. She searched her room for her demon. Garnet Rose was nowhere to be found. She used her magic to bring her back, but her magic wasn't there.

"Damnit! What the fuck did that witch bitch do to me?"

She had one more spell to try. She wasn't sure it would work but she had to try. There was one person she needed most right now.

"Ancient powers that bind.
Ancient powers that break.
Connect me to one that is dead.
Link my soul to hers.
Rae."

An image appeared in the mirror. It was Rae.

"Z. How in the hell did you call me? I didn't think it was possible."

"Shh, Rae. I need you but I'm not sure I'm doing things right. I found a witch to teach me dark magic, but I don't think she will give me what I need. I need you. My light is dying. She's doing something to me… and he's back."

Rae looked back at her from the mirror. She missed her best friend.

"Who is back?"

"Him. The Tall Dark Man. He's back. I haven't seen dad in a while and Nimue left to get help but she's not back yet. I'm all alone."

"WHOA! Z – what the hell did you do all that for?"

"You told me to."

"I know what I said but… the Tall Dark Man is back? What about the queen? Where is Amber?"

"I don't know. I know you are dead, but is there a way you can help me? I need my dad."

Rae was silent, but then she said something that made Z feel guilty.

"I don't know if I can, but I will help you. But I didn't want you to be trapped. Are you trapped? You need your magic."

"I know. I think I lost my light."

Rae laughed. "You never lose your light. You just misplaced it. My mom taught me that your light is always with you, no matter what dark road you may wander down. You need to just find it within yourself. Or did you place it somewhere?"

Zaraquel thought for a moment. "My demon. The demon I created that would protect me. I named her Garnet Rose."

Before Rae disappeared, she said, "Find her. I will find your dad."

Zaraquel had to think about the right chant to bring Garnet Rose to her. Before she could bring her back, the witch entered her room.

Barely feigning annoyance, Zaraquel said, "Geez, you could knock, you know. My body is older now. I need privacy. I'm not eighteen anymore."

"Dearie, we need to practice your spell. You are close to the end. Are you ready?"

Anne extended her hand, and Zaraquel had no choice but to take it. Anne led her to the room where they'd been practicing the spells. She nicknamed it the "magic spell room" because the books were there, a picture of the Tall Dark Man, and lots of potion bottles. The cauldron was in the other room because it needed the fire pit. This room gave her the creeps because the jars that sat on the shelves were filled with things Zaraquel didn't even want to know. She remembered Anne telling both her and Nimue that this was the most important room in the cottage because it was the heart of the magic in the dark forest and a sacred place to speak to the master. *Ugh, the mere thought of the Tall Dark Man sends shivers down my spine.*

Zaraquel practiced one more spell, following the witch's instructions. She couldn't bring Garnet Rose forward in time, but she managed to whisper a side spell. The spell would send Garnet Rose, wherever she was, to her father. She didn't think her mother would understand because her father would need saving first. Her mother was always with the queen. Zaraquel completed her side spell and finished the witch's spell.

Zaraquel began to weaken. She needed to sit down.

Anne made her a drink and said, "Drink this, little angel. You will feel better soon. Remember, you need to balance both sides of magic. The light is within you, but the dark I can teach. It is up to you to balance and choose your destiny."

Zaraquel took the drink even though a tiny spark inside her told her not to. She drank it. It tasted funny.

"What did you give me, Anne? I feel so weak."

"Nothing dearie, but a hot tea. You must rest again."

Zaraquel nodded and did as she was told. Any will to resist the witch was gone. She knew something was wrong. All she wanted was her father.

"Daddy, I need you." Even though she whispered the words, she knew their power. She and her father had that kind of bond. A bond that no one would be able to break. She only hoped he heard her call.

***

Marcus, The Order, Present Day

Marcus stayed close to McPherson while keeping the totem of death in his pocket. McPherson had the totem of life in his backpack. The group managed to keep Nimue unconscious during their journey. McPherson had to make some adjustments to allow Sabre to enter. Rowe and Kabos were spirits, so they could enter with no issue.

Sabre was amazed at the place. Long after the battle of ascension, McPherson needed to allow the group to enter, so he made it possible for Marcus to come anytime. His intention was never to have them separated as he once shared with Marcus, but with all their actions, his family was separated.

He asked, "McPherson, where do we go? The totems join you and me, and I never really got the hang of this place with so many doors."

McPherson pointed to the one door that had just appeared moments before. When the Order was destroyed before, McPherson had to make some significant modifications for protection should anything happen to it again. Previously, the Order looked like a castle because Rowe was originally Merlin and loved his Camelot. While rebuilding the Order, McPherson decided on something different. After all, Rowe left it to him. To the outside world, it was invisible except for those involved with the prophecy and certain special people that McPherson places an enchantment on for them to see. The door would appear when they arrived at the Order.

The Order was a single tower, keeping in Rowe's

love for Camelot, that he believed would serve in memoriam of Rowe. It looked like a single tower from the outside, but once the door appeared and a person entered, the space inside expanded into what everyone would expect as if entering a house: rooms, floors, hallways, and more. The outside would deceive people until they entered. McPherson even set up living quarters designed for privacy between them all. Chloe, Marcus, and Zaraquel had their family-style apartment while Amber and Malakai shared a smaller apartment. Knowing that Jerome was instrumental to them, he even fashioned a spacious yet cozy room for their beloved friend. The Order was always a secret place, but he wanted to provide access to all their allies to protect them all.

"We go there. But blindfold Nimue. We don't want the Tall Dark Man seeing the Order."

Sabre put her down and blindfolded her.

Suddenly Marcus screamed, his hands flew to his head, and fangs protruded. His eyes were red. His fingernails grew.

Sabre said, "Oh shit. The vamp is out of control."

McPherson tried a spell to counteract Marcus's strange behavior, but instead, he lept onto the side of the building. Marcus returned to the ground and screamed once more.

He spoke while staring at the others and said, "This is Rae. Z needs Marcus in the witch's place. I am using the power of the dead to control Marcus. Z is in trouble. Not much time. Save Z before she loses all her magic. Tall… Dark… Man coming."

Marcus retracted his fangs and claws and returned to his usual self, but he didn't remember what had just happened. He noticed the others were scared, but they all tried to talk to him simultaneously.

He broke through the voices and said, "What the fuck happened?"

McPherson laughed. "That Rae. She found a way to get through to you. We need to hurry. Zaraquel needs you. Marcus, are you strong enough? The power that Rae used can have strange effects on vampires."

"I'm fine. We need to save my daughter. I promised Chloe."

Rowe was silent for the longest time before saying, "McPherson, you must study the power of necromancy. We can't let Zaraquel be the only one with that knowledge, especially if evil is after her. There is a legend about the avenging angels. Remember the legend that I taught you?"

"What legend? McPherson? THIS IS MY DAUGHTER!"

"Legend has it that the avenging angels are not just of the highest order and must seek only justified kills to keep the world balanced; they can't fall to evil. Once they give themselves to evil, they are no longer an angel. They turn into something else. I am not sure what since the avenging angels are practically extinct. They have been hunted down like all of us magical beings. There's another legend too. I don't put much faith in it. One legend is about the Hexham line, not by blood to the matriarch witch, but through marriage, in a way. He bears the serpent's mark, but no one has ever seen or heard of him. In fact, we don't even know his name. It's just a story. Let's get inside and I will show you the texts on it. You read those while I figure out what Zaraquel was going to do. Bring Nimue."

Marcus heard something. It spoke to him. It was Zaraquel's voice. She was calling for him. Again.

"Daddy, I need you. I'm sending a demon to you. She belongs to me. Her name..her name is Garnet Rose. Use her to save me. The witch did something to me. She has my light."

He told the others what he had heard, but they needed to do certain things first to save her. He was pulled in two different directions, but leaving now would mean McPherson would have to come with him because of the totems. *Fuck!* Marcus was in pain. He did the only thing he could. He used his connection to Zaraquel to speak to her, though he spoke the words aloud.

"I need to finish your task. We have the totems and McPherson has a plan. I will come to you, baby. Daddy will come. I need you to hang on, just a little while longer. Stay to the light, angel. Learn the dark magic but do NOT embrace it. Embrace the light. I will wait for Garnet Rose to arrive. I will protect your demon."

As soon as he said the word "demon," he received the strangest looks from the others and knew he better explain what Zaraquel had done.

"Zara created a demon. This demon carries her light with her, and we need to protect the demon in order to save her. If you see a demon, don't kill it."

The others just nodded while trying to comprehend what he said.

Marcus stayed close, but his mind worried about his little girl. He had to get back to the witch's cottage, but that would mean they would have to stop their part of the journey, which they couldn't. This was hell.

McPherson interjected his thoughts by asking, "Marcus, is she using her telepathy or a spell to communicate?"

"I don't know. I will ask her.

"Z, baby, are you using your telepathy or magic? It

will be hard for me to come alone because McPherson and I need to stay together for the totems."

"Daddy, I am using magic. My power is fading. I don't know how I know but the Tall Dark Man already entered my mind. Uncle Mac always said to protect my thoughts and the only way to do that is with my magic using words. Will you bring Uncle Mac with you then?"

"I will come as soon as I can. I promise. Keep thinking about the light magic."

"Hurry, daddy."

***

The Tall Dark Man, The Underground, Present Day

He entered Tituba's new room and found her in a spell that prevented her from using her magic against him or anyone else. His Elizabeth anticipated his wishes and commands, even if he did not request anything. His witch knew what he needed from Tituba. Tituba would be comfortable in her room for the remainder of her pregnancy. He looked into her eyes, and the Tituba that was once his was no longer there. She was replaced with something else. Defiance.

He looked at her and said, "You need to drink what's

in the goblet, sweet Tituba. The hunter needs it. As for you, we are through. You will no longer have the power over me that you think. Drink the potion."

"I will not. The hunter can die."

He was seething mad.

"Hunter. My hunter. Your mother needs to drink for you to rise. Show her your power and true nature. I command you to rise, my son. Bring forth your true nature."

Tituba started to scream as her hand reached for the goblet. She would not be able to resist the hunter inside her. The goblet reached her lips, and even though she tried to keep them closed, they opened. The Tall Dark Man watched as she drank the potion.

"My hunter, show your mother your nature."

He waited for Tituba's reaction. Her dark eyes became big, and she screamed, "No! Get this out of me! Get it out!"

He smiled and said, "It will come out soon enough. Rest, sweet Tituba. He will arrive soon."

Tituba was angry but submissive as she said, "How can you bring him forward? This hunter is not what you think. He's… He's…"

"He's my hunter. He was always my hunter. Just this time, a little more powerful than ever before."

"Why him, master?" Tituba started to call him something else but, he knew the spell prevented that. Elizabeth was powerful and cunning and would do anything to protect him.

"I am your master, yes. Only until the birth of the hunter. Or shall I say the rise of the hunter? Imagine what would it be like if the hunter was too mighty even for the queen, and at his side would be her consort, the wolf? The hunter will rise and his dog will be the wolf. It's too perfect. And all according to the dark prophecy. You only have a small role, sweet Tituba, before I am finished with you. Not too much longer."

He used his mind to summon Witch Margaret, Tituba's midwife. Once Witch Margaret appeared, the Tall Dark Man asserted his authority to show Tituba that she would come to regret her choices.

"Hunter, it is time. RISE, my son! Rise and take your place next to me!"

The next few minutes were filled with screams from Tituba. Witch Margaret tended to the birth while the Tall Dark Man watched with elation. His hunter would arrive, and the next part of his plan would be introducing the hunter to his allies.

"Master, master." said Margaret. "Tituba will not survive the birth, but we can save the child. What is your command?"

"My son. I no longer require Tituba. I will summon Elizabeth to assist."

Elizabeth rushed into the room within minutes because of his telepathic connection to her.

"How may I be of service?"

"Ah, my Elizabeth. Assist to save the hunter. I couldn't care less if Tituba survives or not. I do not need her ability to bear my demons or serve me with her craft."

"Master, may I suggest an alternative? Strip Tituba of her craft, her power, and use her body for your future demons. You will have an unstoppable array of demons between her and the angel to fulfill your vengeance."

The Tall Dark Man nodded and was losing patience. He could consistently hear the screams of Tituba and Witch Margaret telling her to bear down. He had never witnessed any of Tituba's labors but this one was most important. Elizabeth didn't have time to assist the delivery because once he looked towards Tituba, he was standing face to face with Witch Margaret and a swaddled babe in her arms.

"My son. Elizabeth, do as you suggested. I must be alone with my hunter."

He smiled at the babe in his arms and walked out

the door.

***

Amber, Honolulu, Present Day

Amber and Chloe decided on a way that might help slow down their current problem. Amber filled Kawika in on the details as Chloe prepared to create a demon. Amber wasn't going to lie to anyone, but she was afraid. She was on the side of light and now they would create a demon. There could be worse things.

Chloe disappeared into the women's restroom and began working on her spell to create a demon of light. The idea seemed so outrageous, but Amber had to do something. Thirty minutes later, Chloe came out with a young woman. Amber thought it was just another bystander. She was wrong once they stood in front of her.

Chloe giggled. "Amber, this is Eve. She's our demon."

Amber looked at Eve and shook her head. Eve looked as human as the rest of them and beautiful but too familiar looking, especially in the eyes. Blonde hair and the deep blue eyes reminded her of her past love. Upon closer inspection, she saw a small birthmark on her right temple that was Chloe's cover's symbol.

Kawika asked, "How is this going to help? We want to get rid of them, not create more!"

"David, silly man. Yes, she's a demon, but she's our demon." She can mingle with the kaimoni and report back to us. The more we know about these Hawaiian demons of yours, Amber and I can prepare the line of defenses that we will need. The only difference is that she's a demon of light. I may have to teach this spell to Zaraquel, if we can ever bring her back home."

Kawika laughed even though he didn't look too happy about having a demon on their side. Chloe went on to explain further.

"Eve will give us the advantage we need. We all know that light must battle darkness and vice versa. All demons have to serve someone. Eve serves Amber as she is the queen. Eve is going to do a little recon for us. We need to know who the kaimoni serve."

Amber shook her head and said, "I get that, Chloe, but really? She looks like Michael but female. What the hell were you thinking?"

"Honestly, Amber. It wasn't to mess with you. But I wanted a demon that I might be able to reuse if we can bring this one close enough to the Tall Dark Man. He might not have wanted to lose Michael, you know. A way to break into that dungeon of his, maybe save my husband from turning himself into him. We're kinda stuck with a demon now, you know? She can't disappear."

Amber groaned. It made sense but she could only handle one nightmare at a time. She said to the demon, "Eve, you heard Chloe. Find us the leader of this demon group, but if you can prevent more people from disappearing, please do so. That is my command. I am the queen."

Eve nodded. "I serve the queen."

Kawika just watched, but Amber could sense his apprehension. She placed her hand on his to reassure him and said, "Better take us to the museum so we can get started. There's nothing more we can do here. We need to trust Chloe's magic. And Eve."

The airport was extremely busy. Amber was amazed that this airport was busier than JFK Airport in New York. When they first arrived through the doors, she didn't recall as many people until she took a good look around the gate area. She noticed something that she couldn't quite put her finger on. There was a large group of people staying close to each other. *A tour group, maybe?*

As the group turned around to leave, the kaimoni must've spotted her because they made a beeline straight for her. Some even pushed their way through the humans. The humans must've thought they were just rude people or in a rush because there was no screaming or anything. Unexpectedly, another large horde started to approach from a different direction and were throwing the humans around like bean bags. And now there was screaming because of the pushing. Amber had to think for a moment but quickly. *Oh shit!*

All hell was breaking loose, and she realized that it was just the four of them, well, five, including the demon, to battle them. Amber wasn't sure about this because just like in Seattle, this would mean exposure. Torn between saving lives, them and the humans, or exposure, she opted to save everyone from the kaimoni. Raising her hands, she sent a stream of fire and lightning toward the largest horde, hitting the wall to avoid casualties. It didn't stop the horde from advancing. She sent a few more streams of fire, hoping to deter them, but it did not. Amber decided a third time might do the trick. However, this time, she focused on one in particular and noticed a monitor on the wall above. Using more power, she aimed her fire at the monitor and sent it crashing right in front of the first member of the horde.

"Which ones are the kaimoni, Chloe?"

Chloe began to weave a spell and called upon the

ancient powers. Amber watched her every movement to shield Chloe from any attack. She could hear some of the words but not all.

Chloe finished and said, "Amber, you, David, and Malia will see them as shadows. I need to weave some more spells. Keep blasting them, just don't kill the humans."

Amber used her magic and vampiric skills to vanquish the demons. She soared through the air, fangs protruding, and ripped the head off one demon before doing the same to another group.

She saw that David and Malia were chanting, and she couldn't stop wondering what they were doing. She could only do what she could to keep them safe. Amber wondered what kind of power they held. Then she saw it.

A spirit stood in front of them. Good spirit or a bad spirit? She didn't have time to find out. Chloe weaved a final spell that sent light through the entire airport, eliminating the kaimoni - all but one. That kaimoni stared at the spirit that David invoked.

The kaimoni spoke to David as the spirit watched.

"I am Kapuni, fallen warrior to Kamehameha. My spirit was cursed once I fell on the battlefield. Mahalo for saving me. I owe you a life debt, kahuna. Call on me when you need me."

Then he vanished.

Amber gathered everyone together. Eve stood among them, waiting and listening. David and Malia were shaken but alive. Chloe, her best friend and strongest witch she knew, was more powerful than ever. Humans were scattered and cowering in corners, children were screaming with mothers and fathers trying to comfort them while others were holding up cell phones at the group. Amber could hear the whispers, "The redhead isn't in the shot. Is your camera working?"

The terminal with the various gates looked like it was just hit by a tornado. Seats were torn and some on fire, tv monitors were smoking, and walls had burn marks, but people were alive. In the background, she could hear the emergency vehicles coming with their sirens blasting, and people were scared. Heartbeats were racing and as Amber could hear all that, her heart was breaking at the sight of the damage she had caused. *Lots of exposure again. Damnit, what to do now?*

Amber said, "This was just a taste of what is to come. I feel that evil has the upper hand. We're separated for a reason, so Chloe and I need to stick together with you until the others can join us. Marcus and McPherson are together, but Sabre is with them.

In order to save Zaraquel, we need to be together. I fear that the Tall Dark Man planned this down to every possible detail. David, I will learn your Hawaiian name, I promise. Our purpose is to help you and your people, but we have a bigger problem. A bigger threat. He's known as the Tall Dark Man, and he is one hundred percent evil. But we need to fix this mess I created. We can't have this kind of exposure."

Kawika nodded and said, "I think I met someone a couple of days ago who might be able to help. Malia will call him to take care of the exposure if he can. Our paths crossed for a reason. Separated is not good for you, that I can see. But consider us your o'hana until the others can join you. I pray to the gods that will be soon."

Amber shrugged and said, "This is just the beginning of a different prophecy, and this time, I fear for us being the ones hunted."

Chloe put her arm around her and said, "There are three standing. The queen, the witch, and the angel. Till we fall, the Tall Dark Man doesn't win."

Kawika ushered them to the hotel, where they began planning for their survival and helping the people of Hawaii against the demons that would come. Amber just wished that her team would be reunited very soon. As Michael always told her, "Let the prophecy play itself out.

Amber smiled at that thought as she started to work out the strategy while Chloe rummaged through some of her books for spells to aid them.

The End

SNEAK PEAK OF BOOK TWO: FATE OF AN ANGEL

Chapter One
Falling

Zaraquel, The Witch's Cottage, Present Day

Zaraquel lost track of what day it was or how long she'd been at the witch's cottage, but there was just a shimmer of red left in her wings. The witch kept a vigilant eye on her and made her practice the darkest of all magic spells lately. That day's spell was to bring a worm back to life. The day she needed was finally here.

Anne brought the dead worm to her and placed the mandrake root next to her along with her mandatory daily drink. Without thinking, Zaraquel drank the tea and started with the spell.

Anne guided her and said, "Listen angel, to bring back the dead, one needs to listen for its heartbeat. There is no beat yet until you bring it back. You know you are successful when the heartbeat is steady. If the heartbeat is slow, the object of your spell is cursed. This is important to know because necromancy is different. You need to be in sync with the dark side of things to control the dead. You do not want to just bring an object back with no control. That's when they turn on you. Understand?"

"Yes, Anne. I understand."

Zaraquel was losing her willpower, her strength. She could feel that she was almost under the full control of the witch. She never wanted this, but her father never came. Why? Something must've happened to him, and she was all alone. Nimue never came back either.

"How long have I been here, Anne?"

"There is no concept of time in this forest. But I keep track. It's now been six or seven months, give or take. Dark magic takes time and preparation for your future must be precise. Are you ready to try your spell now?"

She nodded. She said the incantation, embraced the dark magic more than ever. Before she knew it, the worm was moving.

Anne said, "Now listen to its heart. You must control the worm once you bring it back from the dead."

Zaraquel listened. She was in control. She closed her eyes and commanded the worm to wiggle. It wiggled. She did it! Before long, the worm died once more. She lost her concentration on the worm because she got excited.

"Angel, you have it. You are ready for the next part. It's almost full circle. I need you to drink another tea. This tea will relax your mind. The next spell will take a lot out of you. Do it for me."

"Yes, Anne. I will drink my tea."

And she did. She could see the witch. She could hear the witch. But she couldn't do anything more than that. Her mind was blocked as if it was locked in a cage.

"Good angel. Sit right here. Do you remember the spells from the beginning with the picture to link your soul to another?"

"Yes, Anne. I remember."

"We're going to do that now. It's time. The master wants his angel. You are ready to be his. Let's do the spell. You will willingly link your soul to his. Understand?"

"Yes, Anne. I understand. I will do as you say."

Zaraquel could only watch as Anne prepared the room. The table was set with dark candles, his picture, the powders, the blackest rose, and other items. She made her sit in front of the table, and then she saw a picture of her taken some time ago next to his picture. Then there was her family picture that was in her backpack. Her father. Her mother. Her heart cried for them but she couldn't fight back against Anne. A tear rolled down her cheek.

"There, there, angel. All will be made right. You wanted to learn dark magic and I kept my promise. I briefly taught you all I know after I have lived many lifetimes. Now, you must do your part. To become his. There is no turning back."

"Anne. Anne. My family."

"Is there something you want, angel?"

"Is this to be my fate? My fate of an angel?"

"Not your fate. Your destiny, angel. Your destiny. The Tall Dark Man has a prophecy he will fulfill. That is the only prophecy that matters. Now, we must unbind your heart from your family. Repeat the words after me."

"Must I?"

"Yes. Repeat these words. Unchain my heart, Unbind my love. I break the ties that bind me to you, my mother, my father."

Zaraquel took a deep breath and spoke.

"Unchain my heart.
Unbind my love.
I break the ties that bind me to you.

My mother, my father."

A flash of fire rose and burned her only family picture. Tears streamed down her cheeks even more.
"Now say the spell I taught you yesterday."
She gulped. She didn't want this, but her heart was caged, her mind blocked.

"I call upon you.
The face I see.
The picture next to mine.
Bind my heart, bind my soul.
Bind my mind to you.
Eternity will not break."

The two pictures merged into a picture of the Tall Dark Man and herself. Together. This spell sealed her fate. She screamed with her last ounce of power. "DADDY!" And then collapsed.

ABOUT THE AUTHOR

Barb Jones is a best-selling, award-winning supernatural/horror author living in Florida. While she is an accomplished IT Professional by day, she fulfills her passion for writing supernatural thrillers by night. Born and raised in Hawaii, Barb has deep connections to legends, the supernatural, and everything that goes bump at night. Her Hawaiian heritage plays a significant factor in a lot of her writing. Her family roots return to Ancient Hawaii, involving a royal lineage and being descended from a long line of kahunas. Follow her today and see what surprises are in store for her readers.

You can find her on all the social media outlets like Facebook, Instagram, Twitter, TikTok, and her website. Sign up for her newsletter, which hosts exclusive contests for her readers.